RIDE THE WIND SOUTH

RIDE THE WIND SOUTH

John Hunter

CHIVERS
THORNDIKE

This Large Print book is published by BBC Audiobooks Ltd, Bath, England and by Thorndike Press®, Waterville, Maine, USA.

Published in 2006 in the U.K. by arrangement with Golden West Literary Agency.

Published in 2006 in the U.S. by arrangement with Golden West Literary Agency.

U.K. Hardcover ISBN 1–4056–3640–8 (Chivers Large Print)
U.K. Softcover ISBN 1–4056–3641–6 (Camden Large Print)
U.S. Softcover ISBN 0–7862–8437–4 (British Favorites)

The text of this Large Print edition is unabridged.
Other aspects of the book may vary from the original edition.

Set in 16 pt. New Times Roman.

Printed in Great Britain on acid-free paper.

British Library Cataloguing in Publication Data available

Library of Congress Cataloging-in-Publication Data

Hunter, John, 1903–
    Ride the wind south / by John Hunter.
        p.   cm.
    Novel.
    "Thorndike Press large print British favorites."—T.p. verso.
    ISBN 0–7862–8437–4 (lg. print : sc : alk. paper)
    1. Large type books. I. Title.
PS3503.A5575R54 2006
813'.54—dc22   2005037597

1.

They hung Dave Berry just before daylight on Tuesday morning. Dave was a horse thief, a high-grader and a small-time rustler, and his passing was certainly a small loss to the world. But they did not hang him for any of these things. In fact, they did not actually mean to hang him at all. They were trying to make Dave tell them what he had done with ten thousand dollars worth of gold which he had lifted from the Losso Stage.

But Dave fooled them, or maybe Dave's neck was made of glass and it cracked when they first put tension on the rope, for the toes of his worn boots were hardly off the ground before he was dead.

Sheriff Barney Glass did not exactly order the hanging, but he made no objection when old man Sellers suggested it.

'Thing is,' Sellers said, as they all gathered in the Cattle Queen saloon on the night before, 'Dave isn't scared enough to talk. He knows the stage driver wasn't hurt, and he figures he's got a better than even chance to beat the case when it comes to court. Thing for us to do is to pull a fake lynch party. We storm the jail just before daylight. We shoot in the air like the sheriff is defending the place, and then we take Dave out and put a rope

1

around his neck. We give him a chance to tell us where he hid that gold. If he don't talk we tighten the rope until his toes are just touching and give him one last chance. He'll talk then.'

But Dave hadn't talked, and as they cut him down the make-believe lynchers stared uneasily at each other. They had killed a man. Not that they had meant to kill him. Had they intended it, they would not have felt so badly about it, because there were men in the group who had killed ruthlessly in the past and who would kill again in the future.

But at the moment they were conscience-stricken, which was the reason why no one made any move when Dave's wife took her son and left town.

She was a tall woman, gaunt and unpleasing in her faded dress, a mountain woman who had somehow endured eighteen years of marriage to Dave. Where she was going no one knew, and no one bothered to ask. Only after she and the boy had been gone for several hours did it dawn on anyone that they might know where the gold was hidden.

Sheriff Glass did not hold much with the idea. 'She didn't have no chance to talk to Dave after he was arrested,' the sheriff said. 'I made right sure of that.'

'But the boy did,' said Sellers. 'I caught him around by the window of the jail talking to Dave last night. I personally put my boot in his pants and drove him away, but he probably found out where Dave stashed my gold.'

They considered, looking from face to face. It took another hour before someone suggested that they ride after the widow and her son, and bring them back. And by that time it was too late, the woman was already dead.

*   *   *

There were only three Apaches, bronchos who had broken away from the reservation and were heading southwest in an effort to reach Victorio who, rumor had it, was in Mexico. They were without horses and their moccasins were thin, and their copper-colored bodies ribby with hunger. They had one gun among them, only a dozen heavy lead balls, and not enough powder for a dozen shots.

They wanted horses. They might even have let the woman and boy pass if they had been afoot, since they knew that the town was close and at the moment they wanted little save to escape.

But the two horses were sufficient to make the eye of any roving Indian glisten. They were mustangs, showing traces of both Barb and Arab from which they sprang, inbred and runty, but still the type of horse the Apache knew and understood.

The woman was riding ahead, the boy

3

behind her on the narrow trail as it wound upward along the floor of the rocky canyon. The Indians were above, and the Indians wanted those horses but they did not want them dead.

The first shot knocked the woman completely out of her saddle. It came with stunning suddenness, without warning. The boy was fifteen, big for his age, nearly a man in size. He rode his father's battered saddle, with his father's rifle in the boot and a gunbelt strapped around his narrow waist.

He had no chance to use either, for the shot spooked his horse and it dashed wildly past the woman fallen on the trail, following the riderless mount which raced upward toward the wooded slopes above.

Arrows made their eerie whishing sound as they sped by him, and the Indian with the gun worked feverishly at his reloading, but before the piece was primed the boy's runaway horse had carried him around a bend in the twisting canyon and out of their sight. Silently, doggedly they set off in pursuit.

*   *   *

The canyon fell away from Ross Belmont as he halted his horse on the high rim and stared out over the ridges of thinning timber toward the desert floor two thousand feet below.

Then he started downward slowly, his horse

following the switchbacks of the snake-like trail as it clung with a kind of desperation to the sheer face of the rocky walls.

Here and there a pine had found rootage in a tiny crevice and reared its head, only to have its upper branches bowed by the sweep of the wind which seemed to blow constantly through this empty land.

For three days Belmont had been in heavy trees, crossing the ordered ridges of the higher hills, at times his pony's feet sinking inches into the wet surface of the snow patches, not as yet entirely melted by the strengthening sun of the coming spring.

The air in this high place had been thin and sharp and chill, knifing by day through his sheep-lined coat, by night through the saddle blanket in which he wrapped himself.

But from the instant that they stepped over the brink of the rim and began the long, tedious descent to the desert below, the air had changed, softening and blowing warmly in his face as if to welcome him back.

He was a man of the south, and the blood in his long, muscular body had been thinned by years of desert heat, so he welcomed the appearance of the south wind as an old friend, sent to greet him as he at last returned to the land which he loved and which he understood.

He came down the first sheer drop and followed the trail through the heavy timber clothing the canyon bottom. The track wound

5

back and forth in short, tangential curves that paralleled the tortuous progress of the lashing creek. The water was near white, aerated by its sudden drops as it fought its rushing way through the labyrinth of rugged boulders, some as large as full-sized houses.

Here, under the arch of trees, the sun failed to reach the ground and the earth had a sour, damp smell, which faded as he dropped to meet the desert dryness. He was half down this second grade, out of the timber now, when a single shot echoed upward from the land below, followed by the drum of running hoofs.

At once Belmont checked his mount, swinging it aside out of the worn marks of the trail to find a shelter behind the elbow of a tumbled-rock ledge. As he turned he jerked the rifle free of its boot, swinging it upward, resting it across the crook of his arm.

Both gestures were instinctive, born of years of trouble and experience. His eyes, grey, looking very light in the wind-burned mask of his lean face, were steady and alert and expressionless, watching the curve of jutting rock below him.

First a riderless horse plunged into view, to be followed almost at once by a mounted boy, crouched low in the saddle, sawing desperately at the reins.

A single look told Belmont that the boy's horse was running away, but he made no move to draw out into its path. His measuring eye had already shown him that the breast of the sharply rising grade would slow the horses to nearly check them by the time they reached his place of concealment.

He held his position, as unmoving as a statue, his rifle ready, his eyes on the turn behind the boy, watching for possible pursuit.

The horses came on, the riderless one surging ahead as the boy's weight and efforts checked the second runaway, so that the free horse passed Belmont first, a good ten yards before the second. And then, as the boy lugged by, Belmont had his answer, for a feathered shaft was buried in the horse's laboring flank.

Belmont, who had been about to accost the boy, held his peace, letting the horses go by him, his attention now riveted on the bend around which they had dashed.

He saw the first Indian appear, hesitate, then trot dog-like up the trail as if reassured that no harm awaited him above. A second came, and then a third, and Belmont held his fire until the first was hardly twenty yards away.

He wanted to make certain that these three were alone, and not merely the scouts of a larger war party. The first two carried bows and arrows, the third a Spencer of uncertain date.

Belmont was very deliberate. He chose the

7

third Indian first, the one with the gun, the one farthest away, the one who might have the best chance to reach cover.

He brought the rifle up slowly, carefully, and squeezed away his shot as soon as the sights centered on his mark. He did not even see the brave throw up his hands. Already he had lowered the barrel a trifle, and before the second runner realized what had happened Belmont sent the next bullet crashing into the man's chest.

The nearest Indian stopped, dead still, and then with a howling cry charged directly at the rocks behind which Belmont had found shelter. He moved so swiftly that his gaunt face was already peering over the rocks before Belmont's third bullet smashed it utterly.

His smoking rifle still gripped in one hand, Belmont swung his horse out into the trail. The animal was too well schooled to flinch at the sound of rifle fire or to be startled by any move its master made.

Above them by some three hundred feet the boy had sawed his mount to a halt and pulled the old rifle from the boot, and sat staring, surprise mirrored on his narrow, freckled face.

'How many were there, Kid?' Belmont called, and had to wait a minute before he got his reply.

'I only saw three.'

Belmont nodded, and kneed his horse over

toward the man he had shot last.

The smell of blood made the horse shy a little and he spoke to it sharply, steadying it with a tightening of the reins. Then he looked downward, taking in the outline of the pitifully thin body, the worn moccasins, the long, filthy hair.

He felt no elation, no compassion. He viewed the man he had just killed with the same detachment as if he had been a desert reptile. He had killed because the killing was necessary. He was wary because life in this desert country only continued if you were wary.

He did not seem to be conscious that the boy was riding slowly down behind him. His eyes were now on the curve in the trail, and the folded, sun-blanketed rock slopes behind and above it.

Nothing moved, no unwarranted sound broke the quiet. But still he did not relax. His eyes had read its story from the body and he would have been willing to bet that there had been only three Indians, renegades from the reservation. Yet such a bet would have meant that his life was at stake and he wanted to be sure.

The boy was at his side now, breathing a little noisily through his nose, carrying the weight of the rifle a little awkwardly across the bow of his saddle.

He said slowly, 'They got Ma.' He said it

without much feeling, as if the full meaning of events had not entirely reached his consciousness. 'They shot her out of the saddle.'

'Sure she's dead?'

The boy was not certain of anything.

'Maybe we'd better have a look.' Ross Belmont did not wait for an answer. He rode forward then, around the bend in the trail, still careful, still watching the hillsides which rose from the canyon bottom toward the rims above.

Nothing moved, nothing startled him, and as Ross would have said if someone had asked him, he did not smell Indian. This did not actually refer to a sensitive nose, but rather to an instinctive feeling for danger which was part and parcel of the man.

He reached the woman's side and swung down, looping the reins about the wrist of the hand which still held the rifle and bending downward. He turned her twisted body slightly, looked at the unlovely weathered face, and saw that the bullet had taken her directly in the side of the head. He had his answer. He straightened and heard the boy say, 'She's dead?' and nodded without speaking, his eyes again searching the canyon's sloping walls for movement which might spell danger.

The boy said nothing. His face got a tighter, pinched look, but there were no tears in his blue eyes. Ross Belmont turned from his inspection of the canyon sides.

'Where do you live, Kid?'

'Toprock.'

'Your daddy there?'

'The dirty bums hung him this morning.'

Ross Belmont seldom showed surprise, but he showed it now. 'Hung him? What for?'

The boy moistened his dry lips with the tip of his tongue. 'They said he held up the stage.'

'Did he?'

The boy stared at the man. His blue eyes seemed to be a little close together on each side of his rather high-bridged nose. They looked at Belmont and then fell away, and his muttered answer was so low that Belmont had difficulty hearing it. 'I wasn't with him.'

Belmont thrust the rifle into his saddle boot. He said evenly, 'What kind of an answer is that?'

The boy was sullen. 'What do you want me to say?'

'The truth.'

'Hell with you.'

Belmont looked at him sharply, then away. 'All right. Be seeing you.' He put his foot into the stirrup and swung up. The boy's eyes widened.

'Where you going?'

'About my business,' said Belmont. 'I only help my friends.'

He turned his horse. Behind him he heard a

11

sound. It might have been a cough, or even a sob. He could not be sure.

'Mister.'

He halted. 'What is it?'

'Would you help me catch her horse? Would you help me put her on it?'

'I asked you a question.'

'All right.' The words came out of the boy with a rush. 'So he held up the stage. That's what they said, though they didn't prove it. They didn't prove nothing. They just took him out and hung him until he was dead. Damn them. I'll kill every one of them.'

2.

The town of Toprock was hardly a town at all. A collection of cabins and huts, irregularly spaced, without a true main street, it stood at the head of the St. George basin, boasting a general store, a blacksmith shop and a saloon.

It was high enough to be in the edge of timber, yet low enough to escape the deep snow which blanketed the higher ridges during the winter months.

Four miles below it, where the railroad cut the richer ranch lands of the basin, the town of Stanton showed the square pattern of its crisscrossed streets, a true town and a fairly wealthy one. The people of the lower

12

metropolis looked with suspicion and distrust upon the inhabitants of Toprock.

Stanton was the county seat and it was said openly on its streets and in its offices and in its saloons that most of the rustling, the high-grading and the robbery which happened in the county was the work of Toprock's citizens.

True, they were a poor bunch, living in a squalor not far removed from an animal's existence. True, they kept to themselves, dodging contact with the people of the lower basin, but not all of them were thieves.

The sun was low over the western ranges when Ross Belmont and the boy rode down Toprock's grass-stifled, crooked street, leading the horse bearing the dead woman.

They rode in silence. Belmont had caught the horse and tied the woman's body across the saddle of the unwilling animal. Then he had thrown the three Indians into a rock crevice, since he lacked a shovel, and covered their bodies with stones.

Afterward, following the boy, he had ridden the side trail which led from the canyon across the hills and into Toprock from the rear.

The conversation during the ride had been brief, since in most spots the trail was too narrow for them to ride abreast. He had learned that the boy's name was Dave, that he had been named for his father, and that he had a fierce resentment against the men he considered his father's murderers.

13

The boy would not admit that he knew what his father had taken from the stage. He would not tell Ross where he and his mother had been headed when the Indians attacked. Certainly they had not been coming to Toprock, since a clear, marked trail led upward from the lower town, only four miles away, while they had covered a good twenty in the trip across the hills.

They came along the street and paused before a weathered cabin, and the boy dismounted, crossing the yard to the rear and returning with a shovel.

He spoke then for the first time in nearly an hour. 'I'll get John,' he said, and moved to the larger cabin which housed the general store.

He came back with a fat man whose round head was almost innocent of hair, and without any introductions then led the way to the unfenced cemetery at the end of the street.

John puffed a little as he walked, as if his breathing equipment was not functioning properly. He found a clear space between two plots marked by board markers and said to Ross, 'Dig here.'

Ross dug. The ground was moist from the spring rains, and there were not too many stones. He wondered if the cemetery site had been selected because it offered easy digging in contrast to most of the rocky soil around it. The hole grew. He was not conscious that a small crowd had collected, until he judged that the hole was deep enough and climbed from it.

There were about a dozen people present, faded women and hangdog men who refused to meet his eye. Someone had lifted Mrs. Berry's body from the horse and wrapped it in a blanket, and as he turned he saw a large, black-haired man coming along the street carrying a plain box on his shoulder.

Although the boards were not newly sawed, the whip marks still showed on the unplaned surface. He judged that the lumber had been salvaged from some building for this purpose, and stepped forward, intending to help.

But he was brushed aside by the black-haired giant who, with the help of two men, placed the body in the box, nailed down the cover and then lowered it into the freshly made hole.

Afterwards they stood silent, heads bowed as John read a passage from a tattered Bible which he had produced from beneath his belt. Then the dirt was being thrown into the hole and the crowd turned away, going as silently as they had come, leaving John, the boy, the black-haired giant who was filling the grave, and Ross Belmont alone in the cemetery. No one spoke until the grave was mounded, then John turned.

His face was broad and had a certain cherubic quality. The rolls of fat had puffed his cheeks until they partly obscured his eyes and made them seem smaller than they actually were. They were small enough, too small for the rest of him, and they had a peering quality which was somehow disconcerting.

'Stranger,' he said, 'the boy told me what you did. My thanks to you. It ain't everyone who would come out of his path so far to help poor folks in their troubles.'

Belmont half expected the storekeeper to extend his hand. But John did no such thing. He stood, a kind of pouting look about his lips suggesting that he would have liked to smile but thought it would not be proper under the circumstances. 'You are headed for Stanton, no doubt?'

'Never heard of it,' said Belmont.

He sensed rather than saw that the black-haired giant behind him had turned and was looking at him. The man was certainly big, probably a good six feet six, since Ross was over six feet and felt almost dwarfed beside him.

He heard John chuckle and then say, 'That would hurt the pride of our dear friends in the basin, to think that their fair town is so little known that you have never heard of it. But I assure you it is a comfortable place to stay.'

Belmont suddenly got the idea. The storekeeper was advising him to move on. Something perverse in his nature reared its head. It was this same stubbornness, this same

16

dislike for having decisions made for him that had brought him trouble on the trail. That trail had led him northward until he had reached the Milk and had his look at Canada beyond, thence south through the mining camps of Colorado until he came again into a country which was similar to that in which he had been raised.

He said, 'What happens to the boy?' He glanced to where Dave Berry stood staring wordlessly at his mother's grave.

'Why, we'll take care of him.' The storekeeper seemed to want that understood thoroughly. 'His friends will care for him. Never fear on that.'

Belmont was not convinced. From what little he had seen of Toprock he doubted if most of the inhabitants were capable of caring for themselves, let alone taking care of an orphan. He told himself that this was none of his business. The boy was a churlish youngster, little better than an untamed animal, who had not thanked him properly for what he had already done, and who never would.

But something, perhaps natural contrariness, made him say, 'I'll just stick around a couple of days to get him started right.' He was watching John as he said it, and he saw the displeasure grow on the man's face. Behind him the bearded giant spoke.

'No you won't. Toprock's got enough

trouble without strangers hanging around. Climb on your horse and light out while you're all in one piece.'

Ross Belmont turned slowly. One corner of his rather wide mouth quirked with a tiny nervous twitch, and his eyes which had been quiet and unreadable seemed to flame, but his voice was still soft as he said, 'I'm staying. Who is going to do something about it?'

He had no warning. The giant still held the shovel in his big hands. He moved with speed surprising in one of his size, bounding forward, swinging the shovel as he came, aiming the edge of its heavy blade directly at Ross' neck. But as it completed its swinging arc Ross wasn't there. He had jumped backward so that the heavy tool whistled by, missing him by a safe six inches.

The weight of the shovel and the power of his swing turned the big man half around until his side was toward Belmont. Ross jumped in, driving a fist against the ribs, and as the giant turned back, clipped him sharply on the bearded chin with a solid right.

The blow was cleanly hit and would have put a lesser man down, but the big man merely shook his head. He made no effort to hit Ross with his huge fists. Instead he reached out cumbersome arms and grabbed Ross' shoulders, pulling him forward in a choking embrace.

But Ross had been waiting for just such a

18

move. He raised his knee, driving it into the other's groin, and saw the man's eyes cloud with pain and felt his grip slacken. Ross wrenched himself free, again driving one fist and then a second to the hairy chin as the big man doubled forward. He saw the head roll and the eyes glaze and hit him once again as he slumped to his knees.

There was no mercy in Ross. He knew that this man with his superior strength could break him, snapping his spine like a twig, and he knew also that there was no mercy in the brute. He brought his knee up as the man fell, drove it into his victim's neck, and saw the bearded one turn and drop on his side. Then Ross swung around just as the storekeeper, John, was bringing a heavy gun up from his waist.

Ross was quartered to the man. He would have had to swing clear around and draw his gun before John could fire. He did not try. He launched himself in a spring, using the point of his hard shoulder as a ram. It struck the fat man directly in the chest and he went backward, the gun slipping from his awkward fingers, Ross falling on top of him.

The force of the fall and the weight of Ross' body drove the wind out of John. He lay there gasping, his heavy face gaining a purple look, and behind them someone laughed.

Ross Belmont rose then, rolling over and coming up onto his feet in one continuous motion as a cat twists itself in the air. His hand dropped instinctively to his belted gun and then he saw that it was the boy who laughed. There was something high and hysterical and unmirthful about it, as if the boy had repressed his feelings too long. Belmont moved over to him and grasped the thin, bony arm.

'Shut up!'

He saw that the boy was trying to stop and couldn't. He did not release his grip on the arm, but he used his free hand in a stinging backhand blow which brought tears to the boy's eyes.

'Shut up!'

The high bray of the laughter ceased, and he thought for a moment that tears would come to take its place. Then the boy gulped twice and said in a strangled voice, 'What'd you hit me for?'

Belmont said, 'You were having hysterics. Like a woman.'

'You're a liar. I was not.' He gulped again. 'It's just . . . it's just that John looked so damn funny lying there.'

'Kid,' said Belmont, 'you've got a lot to learn. You're a liar and a braggart and the meanest little devil I've come across in a long time. What am I going to do with you?'

The boy tried to twist free and failed. ' 'Tain't none of your business what I am or what I do.' He was sulky.

20

'You're right,' Ross Belmont told him. His impulse was to put the youngster across his knee and spank him hard, but the boy was a little big to spank. 'Come on. Where do you live?'

The boy regarded him with suspicion. 'Why do you want to know?'

Belmont said, 'I've been in the saddle since daylight. I'm hungry and tired, even if you aren't. Where do you live?'

The boy jerked his head toward the cabin where they had gotten the shovel. 'Over there. But there ain't nothing to eat.'

'I got some bacon and cold biscuits and coffee in my saddlebag. If that's not enough we can try the store.'

At that moment John groaned and rolled over, then sat up and blinked in a kind of dazed way at Belmont.

The boy said, 'You meaning to stay here, Mister? You'd better not. Bronc Charley will kill you sure.' He indicated the still form of the bearded giant with a jerk of his head.

The storekeeper stood up slowly, feeling his side as if he fully expected to find that half his ribs were broken. He glared at Belmont, did not bother to look at the still unconscious bearded one, turned and started away. At the edge of the path which served as a road he stopped, turning again.

'Get out of Toprock,' he said. 'Get out while you can.'

3.

The cabin was a sorry place, one room with a lean-to kitchen. It had two bunks built across the wall, and the few pitiful possessions which had belonged to the Berrys were scattered across the hard dirt floor.

They had eaten, and the stump of a candle stood held in its own grease on the edge of a crude shelf which ran above the old rusty stove.

The boy's sullenness had slowly given way and now he said in a kind of disbelief, 'You licked Bronc Charley. You're the only man who ever licked him. I expected to see him break you with his two hands.'

Ross Belmont did not answer.

'Where'd you learn to fight?'

Belmont shrugged.

'Some day I'm going to fight, just like you. But I ain't big enough yet. 'Til then I'll just have to use a gun.'

Ross Belmont chose to ignore the last. 'Who's Bronc Charley?'

'The blacksmith. He's the strongest man in the territory. He can bend a horseshoe in his hands until it's straight out. Honest. I saw him do it.'

'What's he doing up here? I wouldn't think there was enough work for a blacksmith in these parts.'

The boy's narrow face got a knowing look, but his eyes were clouded with reserve. 'I don't know. You don't ask folks in Toprock questions. You mind your own business.'

Belmont considered the coal of his cigarette. 'What about the storekeeper? Can he make a living up here?'

The boy snorted in obvious contempt. It was plain that he did not think as much of the storekeeper as he did of Bronc Charley.

'Honest John's so crooked he couldn't crawl down a prairie dog hole, but he makes his. He'll buy anything, anything.'

'You mean anything that's stolen?'

Again the boy's eyes clouded with caution. 'I didn't say that.'

'But John offered to take care of you as if he were your friend.'

The boy snorted again. 'He wants the gold. They all want the gold and they think I know where it is.'

'Do you?'

'I told you, no.'

Belmont was more troubled than he had been. 'If I leave you here they'll find some way to make you talk.'

'I'll shoot them.' The boy was still wearing the belted gun. He dropped his hand to the stock and drew it with surprising ease, considering its weight. 'I can shoot. Don't worry.'

Belmont said harshly, 'Put it away. You're a little young to turn gunfighter.'

'Billy the Kid wasn't too much older than me.'

'Billy's dead,' Belmont said, and the boy flushed, then slowly returned the gun to its holster.

'I ain't going to get killed.' He said this with earnestness. 'I got things to do. I'm going to hunt down every one of them varmints who hung my pa and I'll gut-shoot them. That's what I'll do.'

Belmont slapped him. The blow sent the boy staggering backward half across the small room to bring up with a jar against the solid logs of the wall. He stood there for an instant, his blue eyes glittering like those of a snake. Belmont watched him.

'Go ahead, draw. I'll let you get it clear of the leather, and then I'll break your arm.' He spoke without heat, matter-of-factly, in a tone that held definite warning.

The boy stared at him.

'Go ahead and draw.'

'To hell with it.' The boy tried to turn away with a noncommittal air. 'I don't want to kill you. You're the only one ever did me a favor.'

'You couldn't kill me,' said Belmont, 'face to face. And you won't kill anyone else either if they have an even break. All you'll do is get yourself killed. You'd better take that belt off and hang it on that peg.'

The boy's eyes were furious. He didn't say anything, but his denial was louder than any words.

Belmont took a step toward him. 'Take that belt off and hang it up like I told you, or I'll use it to flay the skin off your back.'

Slowly the boy's hands came down to the old buckle. Slowly they undid it, then he carried the belt across and hung it where Belmont had directed.

'That's better.' Ross relaxed a little.

The kid turned to face him. 'Who are you?'

'The name's Belmont, Ross Belmont.'

The smaller face became knowing. 'Bet you've had other names. Anyone who can fight like you has been on the dodge or the outlaw trail. Did you ever know Billy the Kid?'

'I saw him once.'

The voice rose to an eager note. 'What was he like?'

Belmont hesitated. Actually, his memory of the famed outlaw was dim. 'A skinny little runt. A rat of a killer.'

'I'll bet you never called him that when he was alive.'

Belmont did not answer, for there was a noise at the cabin door and they both swung to see who it was.

A girl stood there. Belmont did not know how old she was. It was hard to tell. She might have been anywhere in her teens. She was not large, and her rather thin body was covered by

25

a wash dress so faded that it was hard to tell what the original color had been.

The dress was tight, as if it had shrunk or as if it had originally belonged to someone smaller, and it showed the swelling curve of her developing figure more plainly than if she had not worn clothes at all.

Her feet were bare and the ankles showing under the hem of the dress were small and neatly made. But it was the hair which caught his attention.

It was very dark without having the blue-black shade that might have spelled Mexican or Indian blood. It was shoulder length, and it fell in a kind of cascade of natural curls that made a full, rich background for her slightly elfin face.

She had shoved her hair back carelessly so that one small ear was exposed, and the full weight of the curls fell across her left cheek to rest on her shoulder.

Her eyes seemed dark in the uneven light of the guttering candle. Her features were regular and small, and her skin had a warm, almost velvet look, put there by the sun.

'Hello,' said Belmont.

She ignored him as if he were not present. He sensed an unease about her, the same unease he had noted in wild animals. He would not have been surprised had she turned and fled into the night. But instead she crossed until she was standing before the boy, and her voice when she spoke was warm and husky.

'They've come,' she was half whispering, apparently afraid that someone beyond the cabin walls would hear her. 'They're looking for you, Davey.'

The boy blinked at her. 'Who?'

'The sheriff, old man Sellers, nearly a dozen of them over at the store asking Honest John where you live. I was there when they came in. I sneaked out the back way.'

Ross Belmont saw the boy turn toward the wall where the belted gun hung.

'No you don't.'

The girl swung to face him like an angered cat, tossing her head to keep the falling hair out of her eyes. 'Who do you think you are?'

Belmont said, 'Ask Dave. Ask him if I'm not the only friend he ever had.'

'Friend,' she nearly spat the word. 'Friend. You're like all the rest. You're hungry for that gold.' She turned back to the boy, grabbing his shoulders in both her hands.

'Listen to me, Dave. You haven't got a friend in Toprock. I've been listening to them all evening, plotting how they would make you tell where your father hid that gold. I heard what they said about this stranger. They were figuring how to get him away or kill him before you told him where the gold is.'

The boy was sullen. 'I haven't told him, because I don't know.'

27

She still held his shoulders, gazing at him with her dark eyes. 'You aren't telling the truth. You have to know.'

'Why does he have to know?' Belmont was standing behind her.

She swung around, and for an instant he thought that she meant to scratch his face. She was as poorly dressed as the rest of the people he had seen in Toprock, but there was something different. She was very clean. She even smelled clean, the odor of soap lingering about her without being unpleasant.

'Look,' she said, and there was a well of deep bitterness in her voice. 'Davey never had anything. None of us up on this ridge ever had anything.'

'So you figure to take the money and get things.' His tone was ironic.

She flashed at him. 'Who has the better right? Dave lost his father.'

'Which still doesn't justify using stolen funds.'

'You talk like a preacher.' She made it sound like an epithet, then as the noise of approaching horses reached them she turned, ducked under his arm and vanished through the dark doorway. Ross Belmont stared after her, hardly crediting his senses.

Slowly he turned to look at the boy. Dave had not moved. He stood, also staring at the dark doorway.

The tramp of horses, the sound of voices

28

loud in the night, roused them. The boy jumped for the hanging gun. Ross Belmont caught him, whirling him away, saying in a harsh undertone, 'You'll get yourself killed.'

The boy fought him, silently, wildly, but his strength was not great enough to break the iron grip that Belmont now had on both his arms.

A voice from the door said, 'What's going on here?' and a small man tramped into the room. His body was thin and his height not over five-seven, but there was something commanding about him none the less. His face was weathered from a thousand storms, his eyes were a piercing blue, and his nose was large and hawk-like above the straggling line of his grey mustache.

Dave stopped struggling, and there was fear in his young face. The small man was followed immediately by a big one who did not look to be much older than Belmont. He wore a star pinned to the flap of a shirt pocket, but even without the badge Belmont felt that he would have known him for a law officer. Service stamps a man, good or bad, and leaves something in his bearing which is not like that of other men.

But it was Abram Sellers rather than the sheriff that Belmont watched, for he sensed that this man dominated the men with him, that it would be Sellers who gave the orders, here or anywhere else in the basin.

29

On Sellers' part he was studying Belmont. The ranch owner had not expected to find anyone with the boy, and one glance showed him that Belmont was not of Toprock, that he was a stranger.

For years Ab Sellers had been the loudest voice in the whole basin and the habit of authority was strong. Yet Sellers was no fool, and as he studied Belmont with a practiced eye, noting his well-worn clothes, his single gun, its holster tied down, he frowned, not liking what he saw.

'Who are you?' His eyes were hard and intolerant, yet watchful, and he shifted a little so that the men behind him could crowd in through the door.

Belmont had taken Sellers' measure fully. He had been raised in cattle country, and in every cattle country a few men ruled because of strength, or the size of their outfits, or their own ruthlessness.

Caution warned him to speak softly, for he was a stranger, without friends, without help of any kind, but a certain stubbornness made him resent Sellers, resent the man's right to question him. He said, calmly, 'I only answer questions when I think a man has the right to ask them.'

The sheriff turned red and said with angry pompousness, 'Don't worry, he has the right. He's Ab Sellers. He owns the Box S and the bank and a good share of everything else in

30

the basin. You'd find out how important he is if you were looking for a job.'

Belmont's tone was mild, but it held a trace of mockery. 'But I'm not looking for a job, and I never did like answering questions, or the people who ask them. I'm minding my own business, Sheriff, so just why should you think you've got a right to question me?'

Sellers had been watching with close attention. 'There was some gold stolen from the stage. That gives us the right to question any stranger.' There was a trace of mockery in his hard eyes as if he were telling Belmont, 'You asked for trouble, now you're going to get it.'

Belmont opened his mouth to protest, but Sellers cut him short, saying to the sheriff, 'I never believed from the first that Dave Berry had the nerve to hold up that stage alone. I said that someone must have put him up to it. Maybe this is the man.'

Belmont stared at Sellers, seeing the mockery, and thought, he doesn't really believe I was in on the holdup, but he isn't certain of me, and this is his way of paying me off for daring to talk back to him. He glanced at the sheriff, and at the men who were crowded in the doorway, and knew that he stood no chance against the odds and that he had played the fool to allow himself to get mixed up in this.

But his tone was calm as he said, 'I rode

over the pass this morning, and I never heard of this country before. I never saw this boy before.'

Sellers' manner changed. He took half a step forward. 'All we want is the gold. Tell us where Berry hid it, and you can ride out.'

'I don't know.'

Anger came up to darken Sellers' eyes. 'Listen, you. We don't like tramp riders in the basin. You can save yourself a lot of trouble by helping us. I don't say you were in on the holdup. I don't even care, but you seem to know this boy. Tell him to cooperate. Have him tell us where his father hid that gold and you both can ride out.'

Belmont stared at the hard face. He felt rather than saw the boy shift at his side. He said, 'Ask him yourself. I've been asking him for the last couple of hours, and everyone in this rat-trap town has been trying to get the chance to ask him'

Sellers looked startled.

'Trouble is,' said Belmont, 'he keeps saying that he doesn't know. I was just beginning to believe him when you rode up.'

Sellers stared at him, his face stiff with anger. 'Lying isn't going to get you out of this.'

Belmont was trying desperately to hold his temper. He knew that if he angered Sellers further anything could happen. 'If I knew where the gold was I'd have gone after it already. I wouldn't be here arguing with you.'

The sheriff and Sellers looked at each other. The sheriff was uncertain, Sellers wasn't. 'We'll take them in,' he said. 'We'll see if a night in jail will improve their memories.'

4.

They rode in silence. There were twelve men in the party, and Belmont could not help thinking that it was a large force to be sent after a fifteen-year-old boy. But he kept the thought to himself. They had taken his guns and roped his wrists to the saddle horn, leaving him only enough play to handle the reins. The boy rode at his stirrup, his wrists also fastened. Evidently they weren't going to take any chances on losing a prisoner.

Before them the lights of the town gradually came into view, and Ross compared it in his own mind with the straggling cabins of the settlement they had just left. The population of Toprock had been strangely missing as they rode out. No cabin had showed a light and even the lamps within the store had been extinguished. Toprock, he guessed, had little use for the law.

He saw only one person as they moved past the store, and he could not be truly certain it was she, for the light under the trees was very bad, but he thought that the girl had crept around the store building to stand sheltered by the corner, watching their departure.

The dust of Stanton's main street was a thick cushioning pad beneath their horses' feet, almost killing all sound, but there had been enough to announce their arrival and both board sidewalks were lined with the curious.

Belmont glanced at the crowd and decided that there must be four or five-hundred people on the street. From what he had seen of it, the town could not possibly boast that large a population, so the explanation must lie in the fact that everyone in the countryside had come in to see the excitement. He thought grimly that they were furnishing as much entertainment as a circus parade, and wondered if all of the spectators would remain to witness his hanging.

For he was certain that he stood in real danger of dying by the noose. He did not know the inside story of Dave Berry's death. He knew only that he had been hanged, and if they hanged one man for a suspected crime there was no reason why they should not hang another.

He smiled wryly at the thought. Yesterday he had never even heard of Stanton or of the St. George basin. He had been following the trail southward with no concrete plan in mind. He would work when his money ran out, but that would be sometime in the future, since

34

his wants were few, his expenses very small. If he had not run into this boy and helped him take his mother's body home, none of this would have happened. It showed, he thought with a trace of bitterness, the truth of something which he had always known and usually tried to follow. A man should mind his own business. He glanced at the boy riding stoically at his side.

In the reflected light from the store windows the thin young face had a certain gauntness, but if Davey Berry was afraid he masked that fear well and showed the world a face which held little except bitter sullenness. The boy, thought Belmont, had never had a chance, and this experience would not help. If he escaped, his natural trend toward lawlessness would be intensified and he would die, either here or in some like town, with a smoking gun in his hand.

Almost no one is born a killer. People kill from fear, from love or jealousy, or because they have been so case-hardened by events that they turn as vicious as an outlaw horse. That was happening to Dave Berry now, as they pulled up before the square adobe jail building and the boy was pulled roughly from the saddle and half carried, half dragged into the sheriff's office.

Belmont followed, a grim-faced man at each shoulder. He offered no resistance, no objection. Inside they were lined up, he and the boy, against the far wall, and men crowded in to nearly fill the room. There were, he saw, about a dozen, but he wasted no attention on any except the sheriff and Sellers.

Sellers worried off a bite of cable twist with his teeth and settled it firmly in his cheek before he came over to face Belmont. The sheriff was sitting on a corner of his desk, his eyes never leaving the prisoners.

'Maybe you feel more like talking now.' Sellers' voice showed perfect confidence. 'Want to tell us your name?'

Belmont shrugged. Only perverseness and dislike of Sellers' manner had kept him from answering the question in Toprock.

'Ross Belmont.'

The older man looked at him with an expression that bordered on contempt. 'Another fiddle-footed rider.'

Belmont said evenly, 'I don't know of any law which says a man isn't free to ride across this country if he chooses.'

'You sound like a bunkhouse lawyer. I wouldn't have you on my payroll if you came for nothing.'

'No chance,' said Belmont. 'I'm a mite particular about who I ride for.'

'How long you been in this country?'

Belmont told him shortly. He told him about the Indians, and about Mrs. Berry's death, and about helping the boy take the body home.

Sellers was openly incredulous. 'You expect us to believe that?'

Ross Belmont shrugged. 'You can check it easy enough. I didn't throw so many rocks on those Indians that you can't send a man out there to see.'

Sellers spat accurately toward the battered cuspidor. 'That won't prove a thing. You could have been Dave Berry's sidekick on the stage holdup and still have been waiting out on the road to meet his wife and kid.'

'I could, but I wasn't.'

Sellers glared at him for a long time, then he turned his attention to the boy, and Belmont heard the words hammering at the youngster.

He paid slight attention. His eyes wandered about the room, measuring the sheriff. He thought, Glass is big and handsome. He thinks well of himself. It's written all over his face, in his clothes and in the way he wears his hat. A proud man, and therefore a dangerous one if something happened to hurt that pride. He was watching Sellers and the boy.

So was everyone else in the room, save a small dark-haired man who lounged in the far corner. He had his thumbs hooked in his sagging gunbelt and his eyes were on Belmont. When Belmont looked at him he winked.

Ross was startled. For an instant he thought that perhaps he had made a mistake. He was certain that he had not seen the man before, that he had not been in the posse which had brought them down from Toprock. He looked again, but the man's eyes were no longer on him. Instead he was watching Sellers with considered attention, and Belmont used that moment to study the man.

He was dressed as a rider, and his clothes showed signs of long usage, but something made Belmont feel that this stranger was not an ordinary ranch hand. There was that in his manner, a certain intentness, which somehow set him apart.

Sellers was pressing the boy and getting no place. The kid, after a few short answers, had lapsed into sullen silence, and finally the rancher swung to the sheriff.

'Maybe if we whipped him . . .'

The man who had winked at Belmont straightened and took half a step away from the wall. 'No you don't, Sellers. You hung his father. That's enough.'

Sellers' old face tightened and he turned his cold eyes on the younger man. 'You weren't asked here, Wolfson.'

The man was laughing a little now, silently, without sound, yet definitely laughing. 'This courthouse still belongs to the county, Ab, and I'm still a citizen. I'll come and go as I please.'

For a moment it seemed to Belmont that Sellers would draw, then the rancher got hold of his temper and said shortly, 'All right, all right.' He glanced at the sheriff. 'Lock them

38

up, Barney,' he grumbled, then stalked out of the room.

They were locked up, the two of them in a solitary cell, the only one Stanton's jail contained. It was about ten feet square, with four bunks, two against each side wall.

Belmont stood for a minute after the grille door clanged shut behind them, then he walked across to peer out of the small barred window. It opened onto an alley, and beyond the alley was another adobe building which he judged to be some kind of a store.

The boy had sunk onto one of the hard bunks, lying on his back with his eyes closed, his thin legs drawn up with his arms laced across his bony knees. He spoke without opening his eyes, spoke bitterly.

'I hope you're happy.'

Belmont looked down at him.

'If you'd let me grab that gun I'd have got Sellers. Yeah, and that sheriff too.'

'And you'd have wound up full of holes.'

'What do you think will happen to me now?'

Belmont said, 'Nothing, if you tell them where your father hid that gold.'

'Hell with them.' The boy opened his eyes. 'I ain't never going to tell them. Let them sweat. Let them worry.'

'Whose gold was it?'

'Belonged to Sellers' bank. He was sending it over to a branch he's starting across the

39

mountains, the durn fool.'

'What do you mean by that?'

'Made no secret of it. Didn't have a guard on the stage. Man deserves to get robbed. But Sellers is all puffed up. He thinks he's the ramrod of the whole country and that no one dares to stand up against him.'

Belmont thought this over in silence for several minutes before he asked, 'Who's Wolfson?'

The boy released his grip and straightened out his knees. 'Claude Wolfson? He owns the Crazy W over at the west side of the basin.'

'How come he didn't let Sellers whip you? Friend of yours?'

'I ain't got no friends,' Dave said angrily. 'But him and Sellers don't get along. He's about the only one in the basin got the guts to talk back to Sellers, and I hear tell that he's sweet on the Sellers girl.'

The mention of the girl made Belmont think of something else. 'Who was that girl who came to your cabin to warn us?'

'Who . . . oh, that's only Mary Lu.'

'Mary Lu. Who is she?'

'Old man Walker's daughter. She ain't nobody.' He broke off as they heard the outside door of the courthouse open and heavy steps come along the hall and into the sheriff's office.

For one startled minute the boy's eyes were very wide and fear was stark upon his face, then the sheriff appeared at the grille door and behind him they saw the smiling face of Claude Wolfson.

The sheriff had a key in his hand. He thrust it into the heavy lock and turned the bolt, then pulled the door open. 'Okay, come on, both of you. Get out.'

Belmont made no move to obey. The boy sat up quickly.

The sheriff swore. 'All right, you heard me.'

Belmont said slowly, 'The last person who walked out of this cell didn't go so far or do so good.'

The sheriff's face became an angry red. 'I didn't have a thing to do with hanging Dave Berry, and if you think I'm letting you out just so the boys will string you up you're wrong. I got a court order from the judge saying I have to turn you loose.'

Belmont turned to Wolfson. 'Is he telling it straight?'

The red of the sheriff's face changed to purple. 'No one ever called me a liar before.' He took a half step into the cell.

Wolfson was laughing openly. 'Sheriff.' The sheriff stopped. 'Don't forget that court order.' He ignored the sheriff then and addressed himself to Belmont.

'He's telling it straight. I got the judge to issue the writ.' He held up a folded sheet of paper.

Belmont was convinced. He said, 'Come on,

41

Kid,' and moved toward the cell door.

The sheriff made no motion to get out of his way. He had the choice of walking into the man or of going around him. His impulse was to thrust straight ahead and use his shoulder to knock the man out of his path. But he read in the sheriff's eyes a hungry desire that he do exactly that. He walked around, stepping through the cell doorway and not stopping until he reached the sheriff's desk. There he paused, waiting for Glass to come up to him.

'Get out,' said the sheriff.

Belmont said evenly, 'As soon as I have my guns.'

The sheriff's lips curled. 'There's nothing in that court order about any guns.' He was standing directly in front of Belmont, the heavy jail key in his hand.

Suddenly Belmont reached out. He caught the sheriff's arm and spun him around so that the sheriff's back was toward him, then his right hand snaked out to lift the big gun from the sheriff's holster. He pulled the gun as smoothly, as evenly as if it had been his own, and pressed the barrel into the small of the sheriff's back.

'I'm real tired of you,' he said, 'and tired of this town. Give me an argument and I'll shoot you both apart.'

The sheriff stirred as if he meant to turn, and Belmont's voice was suddenly chill. 'Don't try it. Just get my guns and the kid's too.

Where are they?'

The sheriff jerked his head toward a kind of locker in the corner. Belmont spoke without turning, 'Get them, Kid.'

Dave Berry moved over to the box. He found Belmont's gunbelt and the one he had been wearing. Afterward he brought out the rifles.

Belmont said, 'Fine,' and nudged the sheriff, still using the man's own gun. 'All right, back to the cell and inside.'

The man said heavily, 'You can't do this.'

'I'm doing it,' said Belmont. 'Move on your feet, or with them out in front of you. The choice is yours.'

The sheriff chose to walk. He watched with smoldering eyes as Belmont locked the door, then laid the key on the desk and placed the sheriff's gun beside it.

'I'll make you sorry for this.'

'You can try,' said Belmont, 'but just remember. The next time you brace me I won't forget that I'm wearing a gun.'

5.

The air of the outdoors smelled fresh and clean after the sour, stale odors of the cell. They came out of the building and paused for a moment to look up and down the street.

There were still a good many people on the sidewalks, but no one seemed to pay any attention to them, and Belmont turned to Wolfson.

'I haven't thanked you.'

'Forget it.'

'What happens next?'

The man shrugged. In the faint light which crept out through the open door behind them, Belmont could see that there was a shadow of a smile on the rancher's face. 'That's up to you. Your horse is at the livery. You can get it and try to ride out.'

'Who would stop me?'

'No one—if they were certain that you don't know where that gold is buried.'

'What about the boy?'

Wolfson shook his head. 'They're watching from up the street and also at the livery. They'll never let you take him out of this town until he talks.'

The boy growled deep in his throat, 'Never mind me.' His voice broke and for a second turned shrill and childish.

'I'll shoot them. I'll shoot them all.'

'Shut up.' Belmont did not put much feeling into the words. 'What if I go to the hotel and get a room?'

'They'll probably leave you alone, at least for tonight.'

'Then what did you bother to get us out for?'

44

'Because I made him.'

Belmont jumped and turned. A girl had come silently around the corner of the building and was standing in the shadows not three feet from him. He could only see a vague outline of her face and had no clear picture of what she looked like. For an instant he had the wild idea that it was the mountain girl who had warned them at Toprock.

Then he knew instinctively that it wasn't, even before Wolfson's mocking voice said, 'This is Helen Sellers. You met her father earlier this evening.'

Belmont had recovered himself, and his voice revealed nothing as he said, 'Our thanks for the help. I suppose you had some reason for acting as you have?'

Her voice was strong and level, and yet not without a certain music. 'A very good one, Mr. Belmont. I'm trying to keep my father from making a further fool of himself.'

The words startled him. He heard Wolfson's amused laugh and heard him murmur, 'Rather a difficult undertaking, Helen,' and heard the girl's retort, 'Perhaps, perhaps. The problem now is to get them out of town.'

'And I suppose you have solved that problem also?' There was still mockery in the man's tone.

'I have. You said that if they could get as far as your ranch they'd be safe.'

'No one ever took a member of my crew yet.'

'All right, come on. I'll get you clear of town.' She did not wait for an answer. It was as if she were too used to having her orders obeyed for it to dawn on her that anyone would oppose her wishes.

Belmont hesitated momentarily. Wolfson said softly, 'Better follow her. You have little choice.' They moved down the sidewalk toward the lights of the livery, three or four paces behind the girl.

The people they passed turned to look in curiosity, but no one attempted to stop them. No one got in their way until they reached the wide double doors which gave on the livery runway. Here four men had been loitering, observing their progress down the street. The girl turned in, and the four shifted forward until they barred Belmont's further progress.

'Wait a minute.' It was a small man with a thin, lean face. His eyebrows were a light reddish yellow and hardly showed against the marks the sun and rain had left on his face. He stood with his hand on his gun, his blue eyes level, challenging Belmont.

'Where do you think you're taking that kid?'

Belmont said quietly, 'To Wolfson's ranch.'

'You're not.' The little man's voice was flat and final. 'I have no orders to hold you. I guess the boss figures you don't count. But the

46

kid stays.'

From the corner of his eye Belmont saw the boy drop his hand. He reached out quickly and caught Davey's wrist before the clawing fingers could touch the gun.

'Stop it or I'll take that away from you.' He pulled the wrist up and, retaining his grip, turned his attention back to the men before him. They were grinning as if they found the situation much to their liking. Wolfson had made no sound since they had halted.

It was the girl who broke the tension, calling sharply, 'Get out of the way, Joe Moss. If you pull that gun I'll personally shoot you.' She was walking back toward him, her own gun in her hand.

He threw her a harried glance. 'Look, Miss Helen, your father said . . .'

'I'm saying,' she said. She kept walking. She would have walked directly over him if he had not given way, thus forcing the three men behind him to retreat also.

'Your father won't like it. He . . .'

'Leave my father to me.' Across her shoulder she said to Wolfson, 'Get the horses, Claude. They're saddled.'

He disappeared into the barn. The boy hesitated for an instant and then went after him. Belmont held his ground. He studied the men, amusement tugging at the corners of his mouth. Their reactions were so easy to read— frustration, anger and an utter helplessness to

47

control the situation. They could not pull their guns since Helen Sellers was in their way. They did not seem to doubt that the girl might shoot even as she had threatened to.

He had to admire her. There were few women he had ever met who would have been as cool and collected and self-assured as she was in this situation.

Behind him he heard the horses, their shod hoofs making a kind of drumming sound on the worn boards of the runway. He glanced back and saw that Wolfson was leading two horses, while the boy followed with the horse he had ridden and Belmont's own mount. So, the girl was going at least part of the way with them. The thought had not occurred to him before.

They were mounted and riding out, the girl on their right, using her slender body as a kind of screen to protect them from her father's angry men. But Belmont did not draw an easy breath until the town fell away from them and they were out on the trail heading toward the mountains which showed dimly in the west.

The moon was a small rind high in the sky, giving very little light, but enough to show him the broad marks of the heavily-traveled trail. They rode steadily but with no urgency, suggesting that the girl was certain there would be no pursuit.

She rode ahead now with Wolfson at her side, while he followed with the silent boy. He heard the sharp, clear drum of their hoofs, and a group of coyotes talking to the star-specked sky somewhere to their right, and then he heard Wolfson say, 'If my crew had been in town this wouldn't have happened.'

'If your crew had been in town there would have been a fight.' The girl's voice carried well without being loud. 'That's got to stop, Claude. I can't have you and father fighting every time you meet.'

'The fight is not of my making.' Wolfson sounded displeased.

'You've done very little to keep it from spreading.'

'I don't crawl to your father or to any other man.'

Belmont glanced at the boy riding beside him. He had the feeling that they were overhearing something not intended for their ears. But the kid did not appear to be paying any attention. He rode silently, doggedly, and suddenly Belmont realized that he must be very tired. Five miles out, the girl reined up abruptly and they all pulled to a stop.

'You'll be all right now,' she said, turning her horse.

Belmont pulled his a little to the side so that it halted her for an instant. 'I haven't had the opportunity of thanking you,' he said.

She looked at him calmly, levelly. 'I don't accept the thanks of thieves.' Then she was gone, spurring back along the track they had just covered toward the lights of the distant town, which showed faintly in the clear dryness of the high country air.

Belmont was frozen in the saddle. He heard Wolfson's chuckle and turned to find the rancher regarding him with amusement.

'She has her own opinions, and no one changes them.' He did not wait for an answer but swung his horse and continued westward, with Belmont and the boy following.

The country roughened. It had been rolling terrain since they left the town, grassland which made the bottom of the basin into a kind of carpet, but now this carpet was broken by swales and little promontories rising out of the valley floor.

The mountains ahead seemed to grow in height, looming dark and mysterious as they came through a mile of near badlands and then into the mouth of a wide valley.

Wolfson's ranch sat in the center of this valley, a collection of log buildings scattered over a couple of acres of hard packed ground. They rode up to a pole corral and stepped down, pulling the saddles from their steaming horses and turning them into the enclosure. Afterward Wolfson led them up to the main log house.

He opened the door and lit a match, and by its uncertain light conducted them along a hall and into a big living room. The match burned down, singeing his fingers. He dropped it, swore, lit another and found a lamp.

In the resultant light Belmont had his first good look at the room. It was a man's home and never had known the gentling effect of a woman. Gear was strung carelessly about. A partly mended saddle stood in one corner, a rifle leaned against a chair, coats and boots were strewn as their owner had left them, exactly where they fell.

Wolfson saw the look and laughed. 'A boar's nest,' he said. 'I've never been noted for tidiness, and my cook never cleaned up anything in his life. You hungry?'

Belmont shook his head and the boy said nothing.

'A drink then.' Wolfson found a square bottle on the end of the table with two none-too-clean glasses beside it. He poured two drinks, nearly half a glassful each, and handed one to Belmont, saying, 'I haven't had so much excitement in years.'

Belmont made no comment as he accepted the glass. The whiskey was fiery and burned its path downward to his stomach, injecting new life into his aching muscles.

Wolfson looked broodingly at the boy. 'What are we going to do with you?'

The boy glared at him defensively. 'I didn't ask to come here.'

'So you didn't.' Wolfson held up the bottle invitingly. Belmont shook his head and the rancher poured himself a second drink, this one smaller than the first. 'So you didn't.' He repeated the words after he had emptied his glass. 'Still, that does not affect the problem. We can't just turn you out into the hills and I doubt that you would be safe back at Toprock. If I keep you here, old man Sellers will think I'm merely holding you until I find out where the gold is hidden.'

'I'm not going to tell you.'

Wolfson laughed. 'I'm not asking you to. In fact I'd rather not know. If I knew, I'd only have to go and get it and turn it over to Sellers, and I dislike the idea of doing him a favor.'

Belmont cut in. 'The kid's had a rough day,' he said. 'Where do you want him to sleep?'

Wolfson swore under his breath. 'Of course. Sorry for not thinking of it myself.' He picked up the lamp and led the way across the hall and into a small room which contained a washstand, dresser and iron bed. 'Bunk down.'

The boy hesitated.

'Go ahead,' Belmont said. 'You can hardly keep your eyes open.'

The boy wavered for a minute longer, then he drew the gun from its holster and thrust it under his pillow. Afterward he took off his jacket, belt and boots and crawled into the blankets.

Wolfson led the way out and Belmont followed. 'Feel like sleep or would you like to talk awhile?'

Belmont shrugged and followed him back into the big living room where Wolfson poured himself another drink and settled in a chair. 'Help yourself.'

Belmont ignored the bottle and sat down. Wolfson toasted him silently, drank and then grinned. 'Trusting little wildcat we have in there.'

'You can hardly blame him,' Belmont said. 'First his father gets hanged, then Indians kill his mother and finally a sheriff's posse throws him into jail. I don't think I'd be very trustful either.'

'Staying in the country or riding on?'

Belmont looked at him, but Wolfson seemed to be occupied in examining the seam of one of his boots. 'I don't know.'

Wolfson lifted his eyes. They looked very dark. 'What's holding you—a chance at that gold?'

Belmont shook his head. He did not expect the man to believe him. In fact he did not much care. 'I don't know,' he repeated. 'If I rode on now I'd wonder for the rest of my life what happened to that kid.'

'Rangy little devil.'

'He could go bad easily. In fact I'm not certain it isn't too late, that he hasn't gone bad already.'

'He was bad to start with.' Wolfson said this flatly. 'It isn't his fault, maybe, but his father was no good and the mother wasn't much better. Don't waste sympathy because Dave Berry was hung accidentally. If he hadn't stretched the rope this morning he would have at some future date.'

'Died accidentally?'

Wolfson grinned again and told Belmont what had happened. 'The boys figured Dave Berry was yellow,' he said. 'They figured that once he felt the rope around his neck he'd talk—only that neck wasn't strong enough. It cracked too soon.'

Belmont didn't answer and Wolfson went on, 'You figure the boy knows where that gold is?'

'I don't know.'

'If he does he'd better tell. He isn't going to have any peace until he does.'

6.

The crew was already at the table when Belmont walked into the grub shack. Wolfson sat at the head of the table, with six men ranged along its flanks. They were eating busily and glanced up for the barest instant when Wolfson said, 'Boys, this is Ross Belmont.'

There was an empty chair at the foot of the table and Belmont sank into it. When the cook filled his plate, Ross took a drink from the steaming cup and set it down slowly. 'Kid not awake yet?'

Wolfson looked up. 'He's gone.'

'Gone?'

Wolfson shrugged. 'Slipped out some time before daylight. I didn't hear him, but when I looked in his room he wasn't there. His saddle's gone from the fence and I couldn't see his horse.'

Belmont stared at him for a long moment, then shrugged and began to eat. The food was good and he was hungry, but for some reason he could not get his mind off the boy. He wondered if he had had anything to eat and decided that it was unlikely. The kid would want to slip out as quietly as he could—that is, if Wolfson was telling the truth.

Ross had no way of judging this either. The rancher could conceivably be after the gold himself. He could have had the kid spirited away, perhaps to some distant line camp, while Belmont slept. After all, he knew nothing of Wolfson, and ten thousand dollars in gold would be a huge temptation.

Wolfson had lowered his eyes and was finishing his breakfast. Belmont let his glance wander about the table, sizing up the crew. He had eaten in many grub shacks and slept in many bunkhouses, and he was accustomed to all kinds of men.

This, to his mind, was not a happy ranch. The men were silent, almost to the point of sullenness, as if eating was merely a chore which should be completed as quickly as possible.

They were a slovenly lot. There wasn't, he saw, a clean shirt among them, and their faces were bearded and in places streaked with dirt. But there was something which they all seemed to have in common, an animal nervousness which caused one and then another to lift his head and glance furtively around as though to be reassured about what his neighbors were doing. Invariably, when they met Belmont's eyes their own dropped back to the plate. There was something almost fugitive about it, and he studied Wolfson again with renewed curiosity.

These men, he surmised, had been hired more for their ability with guns than for their knowledge and experience with cattle. He had encountered their kind many times in secluded mountain camps, in the saloons of Dodge and Alder Gulch and Denver, and he wondered suddenly what they were doing here and why Wolfson seemed to need a crowd of hired gunmen at his back.

They finished one by one, and as silently they left the room. There was none of the horseplay and labored jokes which he had seen in so many bunkhouses. The last one left without a glance in his direction, and he found himself alone, facing Claude Wolfson across the length of the littered table.

Wolfson was smiling at him, a smile which held its trace of mockery. 'What do you think of my prize zoo?'

He hesitated for a bare instant and then said honestly, 'I'm surprised. I thought you were running a ranch here, not a shooting gallery.'

Wolfson laughed. 'I'll have to tell that one to Helen. She'll appreciate it. She doesn't approve of my tame rattlers any more than you seem to.'

'I don't imagine she'll find anything amusing that comes from me.'

Wolfson studied him, and some of the humor went out of his face. 'That bothers you—that she called you a thief?'

'Why should it? I've never met her.'

The humor was back, self-mocking this time. 'Better for you if you never do. Better for me if I'd never seen her. I've had nothing but trouble ever since, but I guess she's worth it. You don't find women like her every day.'

Belmont looked at him curiously. 'I judge that you don't think her father has the same virtues?'

Claude Wolfson, for all his mocking ways, was not a man who spoke his mind carelessly, and he took his time as if considering all of Abram's faults and virtues before giving his verdict.

'I've nothing against him,' he said finally. 'An old man, set in his ways, used to ruling this basin as if it were all his territory. But he doesn't like outsiders, and in his eyes I am still an outsider although I've been here ten years. Shall we say that the dislike is more on his side than on mine? I'll bring him around finally. A man cannot hate his son-in-law forever, especially when he has no son.'

Belmont realized that the words held an implication designed for him, that Claude Wolfson was telling him indirectly that Helen Sellers was his property and that he would tolerate no poaching.

He considered the man from a new perspective. Wolfson was not as certain of himself as he pretended to be. No man who was sure of his woman would take the trouble to warn a chance rider that she was already spoken for.

He murmured a meaningless something and pushed back his chair. Wolfson said, 'Wait,' and Belmont, in the act of rising, settled back, knowing that the man at the head of the table studied him.

'What are you going to do now?'

It was a question Belmont had been debating with himself ever since he had heard that the boy was no longer at the ranch, and one to which he had still not found an answer. The smart thing was to saddle his horse and ride away. There was nothing for him here, not one logical reason why he should linger in the St. George basin.

But he knew himself thoroughly. He knew that he would always wonder what had happened to the boy. He felt no liking for Dave Berry, but somehow he felt a responsibility. It was something new in his wandering life, that he, who had avoided responsibilities all his life, should worry about a mountain kid.

'I don't know.'

'Want a job?'

He looked at Wolfson and knew that he did not want a job with this man. There was something about Wolfson that repelled him. It was something instinctive that he could not have expressed in words. Perhaps it was the type of crew with which Wolfson had surrounded himself, perhaps it was the half spoken warning Wolfson had given him to stay away from Helen Sellers, or perhaps it was the man's sardonic mockery which was conspicuous in nearly all his actions.

But he owed Wolfson something, even if it was the girl who had actually arranged his and the boy's release. Wolfson had carried it out and had brought them here to the ranch, meantime making no friends for himself in Stanton by so doing.

He said slowly, 'I've got a little money left. I've made it a practice not to work as long as I don't need to.'

The mocking light was back in Wolfson's eyes. 'A drifter. I had you sized up that way last night.'

Ross Belmont's tone was mild. 'This country is big,' he said in a kind of dreamy way. 'I was raised down on the Pecos and I used to wonder what was up north, so I went to have my look. There's nothing wrong with that.'

'No,' said Wolfson, 'there's nothing wrong with that. A man is a fool to work unless there's something he wants.'

Ross Belmont's response was hardly a murmur. 'I haven't found what I want yet. When I do, I reckon I'll settle down. Until that time, I guess maybe I'll just keep riding.'

'Meaning you're pulling out?'

Belmont deliberated on his reply. It would have been easy to lie, to merely climb on his horse and circle back through the hills to look for the boy. But he was not a liar and he saw no reason not to tell the truth.

'I'd kind of like to find that kid. I might take him south with me if he wants to go.'

Wolfson said, 'Still thinking of the gold?'

Belmont started to deny it, but what was the use? None of these people appeared to have any interest in the boy outside the fact that he might have knowledge of where his father had cached the gold.

Wolfson interpreted his silence as agreement. 'Now let me tell you something,' he said, 'something that you may not quite understand. There are only two conditions upon which you can stay in this country— make your peace with Sellers or work for me. If you go hoot-owling around these hills alone, one of Sellers' men will knock you off. I'm not fooling.' He shoved back his chair. 'Come on over to the house and let me show you something.' He did not wait for an answer but tramped out of the grub shack and across the yard.

Belmont followed Wolfson into the big living room, and the rancher cleared the table by the simple expedient of pushing most of the stuff with which it was littered off onto the floor; then he picked up a rolled map from the corner and spread it out on the table top.

Peering over his shoulder, Belmont surveyed what looked like a homemade map of the St. George basin, with the ranches sketched in. The Crazy W, he saw, ran along the foothills, a rather narrow strip several miles wide and curving as it followed the breast of the climbing mountains.

According to the map, five other outfits dotted the basin and the Box S, Sellers' brand, was the largest of them all.

Wolfson studied the ink lines for several minutes in silence, then turned. 'When I first bought this place ten years ago, everyone in the basin thought I was crazy. My range isn't big, and that strip of clay we rode through last night has washed and eroded until it is nothing but badlands. I'm hemmed in. My cattle can't get out onto the floor of the basin proper without crossing through the pot-holes, and they won't cross.'

'I see.' Belmont did not see, but he sensed that the man expected him to say something.

'Do you? I doubt it. Those badlands act exactly like a fence. They keep my cattle from working down into the basin and mingling with the other herds, but they also keep Sellers and the rest of the outfits around Stanton from working up my way, and behind me there are a million acres of summer feed in the hills. When this country was first settled up for cattle the Indians were roaming free. A man kept his cattle as near home as he could. If they got into the hills, into the timber, he never saw them again, but times are changing. Most of the Indians are on reservations. The few that break out now and then aren't interested in cattle. They may steal a few horses, but nothing more.'

He stopped and regarded Belmont with his bright, mocking eyes. 'I've been a little frog in a little puddle,' he said, and there was bitterness mixed with his mockery. 'But it's different now. The men below me are running out of range. To the south there's nothing but the desert. You couldn't feed one critter on a hundred acres. To the east there's no water. The hills are rocky and nearly bare. You came down from the north. The trail leads from the rim, but you couldn't work cattle up it, and once you did there'd not be enough feed on top to put back the weight you walked off them climbing up. Now do you understand?'

Belmont was not entirely certain that he did.

'The range is mine,' Wolfson said, and there was a sudden hungry glitter in his eyes. 'I don't suppose you noticed, but I've gone up this creek beside the house and run out laterals. I've got five hundred acres of the finest hay in the whole section. My beef fattens in the hills during the summer, and what I don't ship I can graze or feed along the foot of the hills, depending on the season. I've got it made. I only need to hang on to it.' As he spoke he raised one hand to hold it out before him, and closed the fingers slowly. 'I've got it and now, damn them, they are trying to take it away from me.'

Belmont stared at him. 'Who are?'

'Sellers, and the rest of the men in the basin. Two weeks ago they drove a mixed herd along the trail from town. I heard about it, and my crew was ready, waiting. Old Sellers rode out himself. He said that they only wanted passage over my land, that feed was short and they were throwing feeders up into the hills for the summer. They didn't do it. I turned them back, and I'll keep turning them back.'

He stopped abruptly, as if he had said it all, as if he could think of nothing more to say. He

63

picked up the map and rolled it with care, returning it to its corner. 'That's why I keep a tough crew.' He spoke without turning. 'That's why I'm offering you a job.'

Belmont was a little startled by this last. 'Why me?'

'I sized you up at the jail last night. I got the idea that you are fairly honest, which is more than I can say for most of my men. I also got the idea that you could take care of yourself and any trouble which might come your way. I need a foreman.'

This last was so unexpected that Belmont drew a long breath before he said, 'I don't get you. I'm a stranger. By my own account I'm fiddle-footed, and certainly I've made few friends in this basin.'

'That last is a recommendation, so is the fact that you are a stranger. I've been acting as my own straw boss, and it's too much of a job. I can't be in every place at once, and I can't appoint any one of the crew without the others getting jealous. They're a tough bunch, but they're small-time or they wouldn't be working for me, and most of them are none too bright. I'll pass the word that you're tough. You may have to lick one or two of them, but once you do they'll take your orders.'

'Sorry.'

Wolfson said, 'Then ride out of the country. There's something else I haven't mentioned. The people up at Toprock make a good thing of my beef. That's going to stop if I have to burn the place and drive every brush-jumper out of the hills. I can't fight Sellers and his friends on one side and have that bunch of coyotes from Toprock snapping at my heels. Everyone who can't show real business in this territory is going to get out, and that means you too. You are either for me or against me. Just keep that in your mind.'

7.

The sun was half way to the sky crest as Ross Belmont rode out of the ranch yard. He glanced back, just before the turn which would take him into the hills to the south. Claude Wolfson was standing on the ranch porch, a hatless figure that did not stir to answer Belmont's wave.

Two punchers were shoeing a horse beside the open forge, and the cook appeared to dump his slops into the yard. Belmont turned back and let his horse climb the path which Wolfson had told him he would find winding across the hills.

'A way of avoiding Stanton,' the rancher had said. 'No need to hunt trouble when you don't have to.'

Belmont let his horse find its own way upward as his mind considered the man he had left. He had known many men like Claude Wolfson, some good, some bad—men driven by an ambition to own things, to be the biggest in their country.

Ross Belmont had no aversion to owning things, and he felt that when the time came he too would put down roots and build for himself a spread that would be sufficient for his needs. But the drive for bigness was not in him. He wanted only his fair share and no more.

All up and down the trail he had seen the same thing happening, men struggling, not against nature as they should, but against each other, driven by an unseen urge which made them at times lie and cheat and steal so that they might be the biggest, the most powerful in their corner of the land.

Wolfson had this drive. He was chafing under the knowledge that for years he had been only second best in this basin, and now that opportunity seemed to be knocking at his door he was importing gunfighters to keep his neighbors from sharing the range which was not his at all but open public land.

The trail led higher, crossed the military ridge and dropped down in a canyon beyond. This was a land of wild beauty, of rushing streams and lush mountain meadows. Snow still lingered here, a kind of storehouse for moisture which would be very welcome in the hot dry months to come.

Belmont climbed to the jutting of the second ridge, and here he pulled his horse from the trail and sent him along the uncharted course where no mark showed that any animal had traveled before.

He found a deer trail after a good mile and took it, since it seemed to be going his way. The land was rough, cut up by side canyons and towering belts of rock which ran like reefs through the thick stand of the trees.

A man could become lost here easily and Belmont, knowing this, set his course by the sun, heading northeastward, now that he had passed behind the Wolfson ranch. He was heading for Toprock on a hunch.

When he had left the house he had been ready to ride out of the country, and even during the first stages of the climb it had still been his intention to get out of the St. George basin as fast as his horse could carry him.

But near the top he again began to think about the boy. If Wolfson was telling the truth Davey had taken off by himself. Where would the fifteen-year-old head? Not to Stanton certainly, unless he meant to make good his threat to shoot both Sellers and the sheriff.

Where else? Toprock? Toprock was home to him, but would he be safer there than in Stanton? Both the storekeeper and the big blacksmith would do everything in their power to make him tell them where the gold was hidden. He couldn't go to Toprock, and yet . . . he had to eat.

And then Belmont recalled the mountain girl. What had her name been? Mary Lu something? Certainly she had seemed to be the boy's friend when she tried to warn them on the preceding night. Davey might seek her out. It was a chance worth taking, so he turned the horse out of the trail to the south and circled through the hills which towered behind Wolfson's ranch, and headed almost directly for Toprock.

Here and there the timber thinned and gave him a view of the basin on his right. He judged that he was nearly five hundred feet, perhaps more, above the valley floor. At one point he halted his horse and, dismounting, crept out onto a kind of observation point.

Below him lay the even pattern of Stanton's streets, a little hazy in the distance. To his right he had a look at the trail which he knew must lead to the Wolfson ranch, although the ranch buildings themselves were hidden from his view by a timbered ridge which ran out like a pointing finger into the valley.

The strip of badlands which Wolfson had mentioned was very clear. It ran like a divider the full length of the basin, its sandy clay surface supporting so little vegetation that it was clearly recognizable against the green carpet of the rest of the valley floor.

To his left, straight as a taut string, the trail to Toprock came out of Stanton's square of

68

streets and cut a narrow path directly northward until he lost it as it climbed into the hills. There was the breath of dust upon this trail, but he was too far away to make out the riders or to know in which direction they were traveling.

There was other movement in the valley. Four men had appeared around the point which barred him from his view of Wolfson's ranch, and rode now into the twist of badlands, appearing and disappearing as they twisted through the series of gullies and mud cones that spoiled the land.

Someone moved in the timber below him. He had only a glimpse, a figure on a horse, almost at once lost in the cover of the pines.

But it alerted him, sending him at once back to his horse. He was, he realized now, a spectator as far as the affairs of this valley went. He had no part of its inner life, or of its troubles or problems. In fact, it came to him that he had been a spectator for most of his adult years, always watching the people around him, without sharing their likes and dislikes, without knowing the warming qualities of their friendship.

He mounted and rode on, more cautious now. He had no desire to run into any chance rider and have his presence on the ridge questioned.

But for all his alertness she managed to surprise him, appearing suddenly around a small rock shoulder to sit, her crossed hands on the horn of her saddle, her eyes, as grey as his own, regarding him steadily.

He checked at once. He had not seen her clearly in the darkness of the street last night, but he seemed to know by instinct who she was.

'Good morning, Miss Sellers.'

She kneed her horse forward then until only a few feet separated them. 'You're Ross Belmont,' she said. She said this as if she had made a sudden discovery that startled her. 'I didn't get a full look at you last night.'

'It was a little dark,' he said.

She was studying him with candor, a candor which he returned. He realized that she must be a little over average height for a woman. Her hair, showing from beneath the edge of the hat she wore, was warm and had a trace of gold in it where the sun brought the brownness into life. The features were even and pleasing without having the softness of prettiness. There was strength in her face, and a certainty without arrogance.

She said now, 'I'm glad of this meeting. In fact I almost rode out to Claude's place this morning on the chance of seeing you. I was rude last night and it bothered me. I had no right to call you a thief, no more right than they had to hang Dave Berry without evidence.'

'It's all right.' He smiled faintly.

70

'It isn't right.' Her way of speaking held a positive note. 'A man should always be allowed to defend himself.'

Belmont said nothing, and she looked at him a trifle more sharply. 'Well, aren't you going to defend yourself?'

'Why should I?'

She was startled by that. 'Why . . . why any honest man unjustly accused would certainly defend himself.'

Belmont's smile widened. 'I think you're wrong,' he said. 'A guilty man might jump at the chance to say a few words in his own defense, but one whose conscience is easy . . .' He shook his head. 'I think not. Besides, I would probably be wasting my breath. You have already made up your mind. What chance would I have to change it?'

A spot of color had come up into each of her cheeks. 'Why, I never heard anyone talk this way in my life.'

'Didn't you? And another thing,' he was finding an unholy delight in baiting her, 'perhaps it has not occurred to you that I might not care whether or not you think me a thief.'

Her voice became waspish. 'Now look, no one likes to be taken for a thief.'

He said, 'You're talking about people who are interested in the opinions of their fellows. I am not. It would not cause me to lose one minute's sleep to know that everyone in the

71

basin had branded me a thief or worse. Tomorrow or the next day I'll ride out of this country, and I don't expect to be back this way again.'

'Then you aren't working for Claude?'

He shook his head, watching her. 'I don't think I'd be happy working for Wolfson. We might not always agree.' He studied her as he said this, but could detect no change in her expression.

'No, I suppose you wouldn't. Claude told me last night that you were probably nothing but a drifter, a . . .' She hesitated, and he supplied the words for her.

'A saddle bum.'

She flushed. 'I didn't say that.'

'But you were tempted to.'

'Well, yes. I . . . I can't understand how a grown man can just ride around the country doing nothing when . . .'

'When?'

'When there is so much that needs doing. Why, look at this country. How would it ever develop if all men took the attitude you appear to take?'

'Lady,' he said, 'men work because they want things, not because they are unselfishly developing a country. Take this basin as an example. Your father has a big ranch and his associates have big ranches, and the one that Claude Wolfson runs is not small. But what are they preparing to do now? They are

72

preparing to fight—not to develop more range, but to grab a piece of range which someone else already has.'

She was staring at him as if this were a completely new conception to her.

'Me, there's nothing I've ever seen as yet that I considered worth the trouble of fighting about. Maybe I will some day. Maybe I'll meet a girl who wants money for pretty dresses and a fine house and kids. When that time comes I'll probably work as hard as the next man, I'll probably brag and cheat and steal if necessary to get the things she needs. But I've not seen her yet and, until I do, a good horse under me, a good shirt on my back and enough beans in my belly are all I ask. So long.'

He started to urge his horse past her, but she halted him by pushing her mount forward. 'Wait a minute. If you aren't working for Claude, what are you doing riding in this direction?'

A certain wicked pleasure came up into his eyes. 'Probably I'm looking for that gold. Everyone else in the basin seems to be concerned with it. Why shouldn't I be?'

She met his eyes levelly. 'Now you're merely trying to get even with me for calling you a thief.'

'No.'

'And they are out looking for the gold. Dad's had riders out since early this morning. They're searching every place that they think

Dave Berry might have been between the time of the holdup and the time he was arrested. But maybe that miserable boy has already moved it.'

He said, his anger suddenly rising, 'That miserable boy, as you call him, has a right to be miserable. His father hanged, his mother killed by Indians, not a friend in this whole country. What kind of a place is this basin anyhow?'

She reddened again under his words and said with a certain dignity, 'I understand that he's as wild as an animal. I understand . . .'

Ross Belmont reached out and grabbed the rein of her horse and swung him around until they were sitting side by side, so close that their knees touched, with only inches between their faces. 'You understand? You don't know anything about it and you haven't made the least effort to find out.'

He drew his breath sharply and said in an even, deadly tone, 'That kid has never had a chance. He's been starved and beaten and kicked ever since he could remember. He belongs to Toprock, and in the eyes of you Stanton people that's as low as you can get.'

She was staring at him, her eyes very wide. 'Why, I believe you love that boy.'

'Love him?' The laugh that Ross Belmont gave was worse than a curse. 'Love him? I'd like to break him with my two hands. But that doesn't mean I don't realize that he deserves

74

his chance and that if he goes entirely bad it will be mainly the fault of the good people in this basin. I'm going to find him and I'm going to beat him until I find out where that gold is, and then I'm going to give it back to your precious father. After that I'll do what I can to straighten the kid out.'

She was still staring at him. 'And you're the one who called yourself a saddle bum.'

'I am.'

'And you're the one who wanted no responsibilities.'

He shifted uneasily under her words.

She said slowly, 'Either you're a liar, pretending an interest in the boy to cover up your efforts to get the gold for yourself, or you're the biggest fraud I've ever met. Responsibilities—why, you take on responsibilities for the whole human race.'

He had let go her saddle rein and they sat for a moment staring at each other, their faces so close that he could see the slight pulse in her neck. Suddenly he had the overpowering impulse to kiss her. It wasn't because he found her attractive, it was nothing conscious on his part, and he acted even without thought.

He swayed sidewise, put one arm about her shoulders, drawing her slender body against his until her high breasts under the light shirt she wore were pressed against him. Then he kissed her, not violently, but a little wonderingly, gentle even with the surge of his rising passion.

She made no effort to free herself, no effort to avoid his lips. It might have been surprise which held her passive. He had no way of knowing. He only realized after a moment that she was not returning his kiss. Her lips were cool and immobile and impassive. He let her go, and for an instant their eyes locked. His were the first to fall away.

'Adios.' He swung the horse and drove it into a sudden headlong jump with a jab of his spurs. He rode ahead then, ducking to avoid the low-slung branches of the trees. When he looked back she was already lost to sight. He never expected to see her again.

8.

Toprock drowsed in the heat of the late afternoon sun. There was very little movement among the cabins. Several men rode up to the store and departed loaded with supplies, while a woman carrying a shopping bag left her cabin and walked the hundred yards to the store building and vanished within.

At the blacksmith shop a wagon had been tilted upward while the bearded figure of Bronc Charley labored at one of its axles.

Ross Belmont watched it all with a sense of

detachment. He had chosen his vantage point well, a rocky shoulder which thrust up through the timber behind the town. He had no idea where the girl Mary Lu lived, and it was no part of his plan to show himself in this town.

His thoughts, usually so ordered, were in a kind of turmoil. He could not forget what Helen Sellers had said to him—that he was taking on the responsibilities of mankind. He thought, she was trying to tell me that I'm attempting to play God, and that it can't be done. Why should I single myself out to take care of that boy? And then he recalled a story he had heard years before.

A prospector had once saved a man's life, dragging him to safety after finding him waterless in the middle of the desert. The rescued man had turned out to be no good, but in some curious way the prospector had felt a certain responsibility for him.

Belmont remembered both men well. They had finally come to rest in the small Texas town where he had been raised. The man who had been saved was in constant trouble, always being rescued by the prospector. Finally, the troublemaker had killed a man and holed up in an old house. The sheriff had been collecting a posse to dig him out when the prospector arrived.

'I'll get him,' he said. 'He's my responsibility. If I hadn't saved him he wouldn't be here now.' He went into the house after the drunken man, and they were both killed in the resulting gunfire.

Belmont wondered if that was the way it was with him and the boy. If he had not come along, the Indians would have eventually hunted the youngster down. He would have been dead, and therefore the responsibility of no one. But he was alive, and Belmont knew that he would never rest easy until he had done what little he could for the boy.

It was beginning to grow dark now. The sun had sunk behind the distant range, and the light was fading fast as it always does the minute the sun sets in the desert country. Lamps had been lit here and there, showing their faint glow through the cabin windows.

And then, when he was about to give the whole thing up as useless, he saw her. She appeared suddenly out of the timber below him, hesitated for a moment, looking about the straggling town site, and then fled, swift as a bird, to disappear through the door of a cabin to his extreme right. He watched and saw a lamp come on within, and guessed that she must be alone, and turned and made his careful way down the rear of the rock thrust, and circled it to come out behind her cabin.

He paused, listening, and heard no sound of voices. He looked again at the town to make certain his movements would not be observed.

There was no one in sight. Lights burned

78

from the store building, but the blacksmith shop was dark and deserted.

He came around from the rear, his booted feet making no sound on the carpet of needles which blanketed the ground. The door was open, and a glance showed him that the single room was deserted save for the girl, who was doing something at the battered stove.

When he spoke softly from the threshold she jumped and twisted, like an animal ready for flight. Had there been another exit from the cabin he was sure that she would have fled. Instead, she backed away from the door until she was crouched in the far corner.

He said, 'There's nothing to be afraid of, Mary Lu. I'm a friend of Davey's. I've got to find him.'

No sound came from the girl and he took a long stride into the room. 'Listen to me. I know you think I'm like the rest, hounding him to find out what happened to that gold that was stolen from the stage. But I'm not.'

Still she didn't speak, but it seemed to him that she was not cowering quite so much, that her young body had straightened and that her breathing was not quite so labored.

'Get away! I don't know where he is.'

'You do. You were with him this afternoon. I watched you come back. I want you to take a message to him from me. I want you to tell him that I've got to see him, that Sellers' men are searching the country for him, and that it's only a matter of time until he's caught.'

'He don't want to see you.'

'I don't believe that. He knows I'm his friend. He knows what I did for him yesterday. He knows that they took me to jail with him and that I'm not on the sheriff's and Sellers' side.'

She did not answer.

'Look,' he said, 'I could go and get the blacksmith and Honest John from the store, and tell them that you are hiding Davey. Do you have any idea what they would do to you?'

Her eyes showed that she did.

'But I'm not going to do that. I'm going to slip out of here in a minute. I'm going over to where I left my horse behind that rock upthrust, and I'm going to wait there until you find out if Davey wants to see me.'

He turned and was gone. He did not know if he had succeeded, and he was not going to try to follow her. If he did, and she discovered him, anything he might have already accomplished would be lost. He moved quickly back into the trees, not fearing discovery now since it was almost dark. It was, in fact, so dark that he experienced some difficulty in locating his horse.

He sat down with his back to the tree to which the horse was tethered. He wanted a smoke, but he feared to take the chance. He was very close to Toprock and some of its citizens might well be prowling through the

80

brush. The smell of burning tobacco might excite their curiosity.

As he waited, Belmont's ears became more attuned to the night sounds as they drifted through the timber, noises of nocturnal creatures and animals moving about in search of food. The thought of food made him very conscious of his own stomach. He had not eaten since that morning.

He did not hear her come and he had no idea how she so quickly found him in the darkness, but although he could not see her face he sensed the strain about her even before she spoke.

'Quick! He's in trouble.'

She turned then, and led the way through the timber behind the rising rocks. Twice she stopped, and her whisper came back to him, 'Quiet. Be careful.'

The second time he caught her arm and pulled her against him so that his lips were close to her small ear. 'What is it?'

'Bronc Charley.'

He let her go and followed, careful as he could be about the sounds he made. Although his progress was not as quiet as hers, it carried no warning to the men above, for both Bronc Charley and Honest John were too engrossed in their questioning to pay any attention to the noises which reached them out of the timber.

They were on a shelf, perhaps a dozen feet in width, which ran out from the side of the canyon like an extended lip. At its base, against the flat wall of rising rock, was a small opening. It was hardly a cave, rather an overhang where wind and rain had scooped out a shallow depression which would give temporary shelter from the elements.

The boy's horse was picketed below the edge of the timber, and the men had built a fire, possibly to see better the face of their small victim.

The boy sat with his back against the rock face, his knees pulled up and his arms, too long for the sleeves of his shrunken shirt, crossed upon his knees so that his overlarge hands dangled loosely without support.

He was sullen, hardly a word coming from him, his only answers a stubborn shake of his head. Honest John was doing the questioning, and there was something oily in his tone and in the obsequious smile which graced his fat face.

'Get some sense, Davey.' He spoke with the restrained deliberation of a patient man who has found that his patience has been tried too far. 'You can't go it alone. No one can.'

The boy did not answer.

'It ain't like we weren't friends. Me and Bronc Charley has watched you grow from a little shaver. Your father now, he was one of us. He lived in Toprock. And who gave him credit at the store?'

'Hell with you.' They were the first words

the boy had uttered since Ross Belmont had come within the reach of their voices. Belmont stood now, a half dozen feet below the ledge, partly concealed by the bole of an enormous pine. They could have seen him had they turned their heads, but the gold madness was on them, and the thought of it was driving them.

John's voice hardened as he said, 'I've tried to be nice to you, kid. I've tried to show you that you can't never get away with that gold alone.'

And then surprisingly the young voice said, 'I wouldn't touch it with a forked stick. I don't want it. I just don't want old Sellers to ever get it. I want his penny-pinching, narrow soul to shrivel up and die thinking about the gold that isn't his any more, and then I'll kill him.'

The words caught John unprepared. For a moment he stared at the boy as if he failed to believe what he heard. Then his fat face split with its ready smile, and he said in his oily voice, 'Why son, I'm right proud of you, that I am, proud to think that you was raised in Toprock, and that your daddy was my friend.'

'He wasn't your friend,' the boy said, 'and I don't like you better than I do Sellers. I ain't telling you where the gold is. I ain't telling no one. It can stay there 'til it rots.'

Bronc Charley's grumbling voice cut in, 'We've wasted time enough.' He pushed John's fat body out of the way and for a moment towered above the seated Davey. Then he bent down, seizing one of the thin wrists, and jerked the boy to his feet.

'I listened to John, now I'll do it my way. I'm going to break your fingers, one at a time, until you get some sense. You want to be a gunman. Well, when I finish with you, you'll never hold a gun again.'

'That,' said Ross Belmont, 'will be the end of the party.' He had stepped sidewise away from his tree, and his gun was in his hand, frowning upward at them. 'You're too big to miss, Charley. Let go the boy's arm.'

Bronc Charley turned until Ross could see his bearded face. His dark eyes glittered in the firelight, and anger sent a red glow into the leather skin above the edge of the beard.

'You again?'

Belmont said, 'Drop his arm.'

Instead, Charley turned with his surprising speed, yanking the boy around with him, pulling the thin body back against him and crouching a little so that Davey's body made a kind of shield.

He grimaced across the boy's shoulder, and his free hand dropped and tugged loose the gun from his holster. It was obvious that he did not expect Belmont to shoot, that he meant to take his time, hidden behind the boy, and make certain that his own bullet went true.

But Belmont's gun had steadied against his

hip. It spoke once, and there was a sudden hole directly in the middle of Bronc Charley's forehead.

The big man fell. The gun slipped from his fingers, and he took the boy down with him so that he fell across the smaller body. Belmont never gave him a second glance. His full attention was on the storekeeper.

Honest John had been reaching for his own weapon. He stopped, his head turning to look at Bronc Charley with a dazed incredulity. Then he looked back at the man below him, and his fat hands came out and up in a negative gesture which was more expressive than any words.

9.

They were alone on the small shelf before the cave, the boy and Belmont, alone save for the dark, silent shape of Bronc Charley's body, huge and mounded under the flickering light from the dying fire.

The fat man was gone, scrambling away like some overgrown crab, pathetic in his eagerness to escape. Not until he was safely into the timber did he pause, then like a vindictive child he sent his voice back to them.

'You'll be sorry. You'll hang for Charley's murder. That's what will happen to you.'

The boy had retrieved his guns and fastened the heavy belt about his slender hips. He turned now and would have gone in pursuit had not Belmont halted him with a word. He faced about, resentful at being checked. 'You don't know him. He's the meanest man alive. He'll do anything. Anything. We shouldn't let him go.'

Ross Belmont noticed the 'we.' It was the first break in the boy's solid front, the first time he had consciously associated himself with Belmont.

Before, they had been two strangers, tossed together by chance. That Belmont had saved him from the Indians, that Belmont had helped bury his mother and then been taken with him to jail, had meant nothing. But now ... The boy turned and walked over to where Bronc Charley lay, staring down at the big, bearded face. He looked up and there was an unwilling admiration in his face.

'Some shooting.'

In an obscure way it angered Belmont that the only emotion he had been able to arouse in this waif was one of admiration for his shooting. He said shortly, 'The target was large.'

The boy came back to him then, standing before him, looking very thin and immature in the uncertain light. 'It wasn't that. He was using me as a shield and I figured you wouldn't shoot with me there, or maybe that

86

you would hesitate and be too late. He almost had that gun up.'

Ross Belmont said, 'Maybe I just didn't care whether I hit you or not.'

'But you did,' Davey said with simple logic. 'If you hadn't cared you wouldn't have come back.'

'Maybe I came back to get the gold.'

Again the boy shook his head. 'No, I saw that last night at the jail. You don't care for the gold any more than I do.'

'Then why don't we give it back?'

The young face which had relaxed a little set in stubborn lines and Davey turned away.

The girl had come out of the trees where she had been hiding. She moved swiftly, climbing to the ledge, went by Belmont and had her curious look at Bronc Charley. Her thin face was entirely without expression as she came back to the fire, saying without preamble, 'Davey's right. You should have killed John.'

Belmont looked at her, thinking as he did so how very close to nature these two were. It was not cruelness that prompted her remark, but a realization far beyond her years of the necessity of certain things for survival.

To her and to the boy, John represented both greed and power. His store, by giving limited credit to the sorry citizens of Toprock, gave him a certain hold upon their lives, and instinctively they feared and hated him.

87

He said gently, 'I couldn't just shoot him down in cold blood. He would not even reach for his gun.'

'Why not? Who knows whether Bronc Charley reached for his gun or not?'

'I do,' he said. He said it soberly. 'I have to live with myself, Mary Lu.'

She did not understand. She knew only the very simple things, like hunger and cold and fear, and perhaps love and hate. He glanced at her curiously. She was, he saw, not much older than the boy. Perhaps she was no older, but being a girl had matured a little sooner. Still, there was nothing of the coquette in her, no half glances that might contain a hint of promise. She was, he realized, interested in him only for the strength he had, for the protection that his gun could bring.

She said, 'You won't live too long if John can help it. He's the boss here, and he won't stand for word to get around that he's been backed down and made to crawl. He'll hate you for that, and hate Davey too, hate him almost as much as he already does for not turning over that gold.'

'And hate you too?'

She shook her head. 'No. He didn't see me. I made sure he didn't. I stayed in the timber until he had gone.' Belmont had not thought of that. He remembered now that as they approached the ledge she had lagged behind, apparently not sure of the outcome, not willing to expose herself until she knew which way the cards would fall.

He turned to the boy. 'How'd they find you?'

Dave Berry stirred. It was obvious that the words came out of him with reluctance. 'My fault. I built a fire. I figured it wouldn't show from down below. I was hungry, and Mary Lu had brought some meat.'

Belmont said, 'Which reminds me that I'm hungry too. Shall we go back to your cabin and see what we can scare up in the way of grub?'

The girl's answer was quick. 'Not to my cabin. I have to stay in Toprock.'

'Which brings up another point.' Belmont was looking at the boy. 'What do we do now, drift out of the country?'

The small jaw set. There was no answer.

'Still figuring on killing Sellers and the sheriff?'

'What if I am?'

'Look,' said Belmont. 'I'll make a deal with you. I can't do what I should, which is to ride away and let you sweat it out by yourself. I'd have you on my conscience, and you aren't something I want to spend the rest of my life thinking about.'

'You don't have to.'

The man had had enough. He reached out suddenly and grabbed the front of the boy's shirt and jerked him forward until only inches separated their faces. 'Listen to me. I've had nothing but sass from you since we first met. You're a kid with a swelled head and some wild ideas. Well, let me tell you something. You're going to take off that gun and stop acting like your idea of an outlaw. This isn't a game we're playing.' He reached down with one hand and unbuckled the boy's gunbelt and tossed it into the bushes.

'You're coming with me. I don't know where, but we'll find somewhere to settle down. And you're going to stay with me for five years—until you're twenty. You're going to learn to mind, to jump when I speak to you, and if you try to run away I'll flay the hide off your back.'

The eyes so close to his were hard and unyielding. 'Then,' Belmont said, 'if five years from now you still feel the way you do now, I wash my hands of you. You can come back and kill Sellers and the sheriff and all the rest you want to. You can get your neck stretched and wind up dead on some saloon floor because you ran into another kid just as crazy and a little faster with a gun.' He shook the boy as if to emphasize the words. 'Now get your horse and come along while I pick up mine. Do you know a place where we can hole up safely for the night?'

The boy did not answer. The girl said, 'Black Canyon. There's water there and a place you can build a small fire if you're careful.'

He nodded and searched his pocket, finding a single gold piece. 'Can you get us some grub without getting into trouble?'

She met his eyes squarely. 'I can steal some. I know a way into John's store. If I bought it with that he'd want to know where it came from.'

Belmont said, 'Keep it. You might need it for yourself. I guess Honest John owes us something. If you can get some flour and beans, bacon and coffee, we'll make out. Can you have it for us by daylight?'

She nodded. The boy still hadn't spoken. Suddenly she turned toward him and put her arms about his slender body and kissed him on the cheek, and when she spoke her voice was softer than Belmont had heard it.

'Listen, Davey. You do what this man says. He means good by you. I don't know how I know, but I do. You go with him, and when you get safe away you write me a letter. You tell me where that gold is hid.'

She turned then, and with a strange gracefulness she skipped down from rock to rock, like a ballet dancer, moving lightly on her toes to disappear into the shadow of the timber.

Belmont had to choke down a sudden, wild impulse to laugh. The pattern did not change. Even the girl was hungry for the gold.

Black Canyon was a gash, narrow and

twisting, which ran up toward the distant rim. A creek had cut its way through the hard, rocky ridge, tumbling water which for a million years had worked untiringly to gouge out this path for itself toward the thirsty desert below.

They rode in silence through the darkness. At first Belmont had been afraid that the boy would try to elude him, but apparently Davey had no thought of escape. He rode in front because he knew the country, and Belmont followed so closely that at times there was no space between the horses.

They cut west through the timber and then turned north, finding a side trail which led down into the canyon's darkness, feeling their way along the narrow trail for what seemed hours, until they finally heard the welcome roar of the water from below and dropped down at last to the stream, aspen-bordered and quiet at this point, caught in a pool behind a rock slide below them.

Here, under the overhang of the wall so that the light would not be noticeable from above, they built a little fire and hobbled their horses on a patch of grass along the stream.

As he dismounted, the boy had drawn the rifle from its boot and he carried it with him to the camp. Belmont noticed this and offered no comment. Not until the fire was built and they had settled on their saddle blankets beside it did he speak.

'So you've made up your mind to go with me?'

The boy did not look at him. 'You didn't need to throw my gun away.'

Belmont said slowly, 'You can have another gun, a better one, when you've earned it.'

The eyes came up then, dark and inscrutable. 'Earned it?'

'Earned it,' said Belmont, 'and learned to use it. As long as you had that belt strapped around your belly, someone who didn't know how young you are might have jumped you. You can keep the rifle. A rifle is different from a short gun. It isn't an invitation for trouble.'

'Where we going?'

Belmont had found his short, blackened pipe in his pocket and was shaving thin slices from the plug of black tobacco into his palm. 'Where do you want to go?'

The boy considered. 'Pa used to talk to me sometimes. Pa said there was a big world out beyond these hills. Pa said that some day we'd get some money and go see that world. Ma would tell him to shut up, to not be foolish. I guess maybe I'd like to see something of that world.'

As he lit his pipe, Belmont had a mental picture of the cabin's slovenly interior, of the man, probably weak, trapped here by his own lack of courage, by his own inability to face the world, yet dreaming aloud of traveling its endless paths.

'Is that why he held up that stage?'

'I don't know.' The boy's voice, which had lifted for an instant, returned to sullenness. 'He never done nothing like that before. Maybe he branded a couple of cattle which wasn't his, but he never held up nothing.'

'Where'd he hear about the gold?'

'He heard Claude Wolfson was hiring and he went over to see about a riding job, only Wolfson wouldn't hire no one from Toprock. He was on his way back when he met the stage, and he stopped it to ask old man Meyer for a match, and old man Meyer is a talkative cuss and he told Pa about the gold he was carrying.' It was more talk than the boy had indulged in since Belmont had known him.

'I guess maybe Pa just went kind of crazy at the thought of all that gold. He pulled his gun and made old man Meyer get down and start walking out across the brush, then he tied his horse to the back of the stage and drove it five or six miles down the road. Afterward he took the box on his horse and lit into the hills. They never would have caught him if he hadn't tried to sneak back to town for Ma and me.'

They were silent, each wrapped in his own thoughts. Belmont thought wryly that the line between honesty and robbery was very thin. The boy's father might have been a petty crook, perhaps driven to such by hunger, but even just before the robbery he had been trying to secure employment. And then, to ride away with ten thousand dollars, a fortune beyond his wildest imaginings, probably opened up in his warped mind the pathway to the world of which he had dreamed.

'And he wouldn't tell them, not even to save his life?'

'He wasn't worried,' said the boy. 'Not much. I talked to him through the jail window. The bums wouldn't let me see him. He said he didn't hurt old man Meyer. All they could do was send him to prison. He'd go, and we'd have the money when he came out.'

They were silent again for a long time, but somehow a certain comradeship had crept into the silence. The boy was lying on his back, his hands under his head. His face in the flickering light of the fire no longer held the sullen cast.

'I'm hungry.'

'So am I.'

'Mary Lu can't get here much before morning. She'll have to wait until Honest John shuts the store.'

Silence again, then the boy asked, 'Did you ever shoot anyone except Bronc Charley?' As he asked it, he rolled over and came up on one elbow.

Belmont's face was suddenly grey, but his voice when he spoke was under control. 'Yeah, one man.'

'Where?'

He hesitated a moment. 'Down in west Texas.'

'That where you're from?'

Ross Belmont nodded silently.

'That why you left home?'

Again the nod.

'Tell me about it?'

Belmont was about to refuse. Something stopped him, perhaps the interest in the boy's face. He thought, I can't expect this kid to loosen up with me, to try to understand me if I shut him out. And maybe it would be a good thing to talk about it. It had been a long time since he had talked with anyone openly and about himself.

He said, 'Just a man . . . We had a difference and he braced me on the street. I couldn't back down.'

'Why?'

'Well,' he said, 'there was a girl . . .' His eyes took on a far-away look. 'She couldn't seem to make up her mind which one of us she wanted. We had a fight and I licked him with my fists, and then he went after a gun. We were both pretty young.'

'How long ago?'

'Four years.'

'And you killed him?'

'I got my gun out faster, and he was down in the dust of the street, and suddenly I recalled that we'd grown up together, that we'd been friends until she came along.' He glanced

96

again at the boy's face.

'Well, what happened? Did the posse chase you?'

He shook his head, and all the grief and heartbreak of that night was back upon him. 'It wasn't that. It was a fair fight. It was the girl. It seems she made up her mind too late. She went down on her knees beside him, and then she looked up and called me a murderer.'

The boy was eager. 'Then what?'

'Nothing,' said Belmont. 'Try to get some sleep.' He rolled over then, pulling the blanket about his shoulders, but sleep did not come. The fire burned down, but there was some light reflected from the eastern horizon.

He cursed himself for a fool. He had consciously through the years tried not to remember, and the galling bitterness of that night had faded in his mind, but now it was back with him, haunting him with sharp clarity.

10.

Helen Sellers ate her dinner alone in the hotel dining room and afterward sought a chair in a darkened corner of the high porch. She was alone, and from her vantage point she had an unrestricted view of most of Stanton's main street. Usually, when she stayed at the rooms

97

her father kept at the hotel for their visits to town, she spent the evening with one of the girls with whom she had gone to school, who had married the owner of the harness shop. But tonight she was restless and felt that she could not face the steady flow of June's conversation.

Ordinarily able to school herself, she suffered now from a rising feeling of frustration which she did not entirely comprehend. Part of the feeling came no doubt from her anger with her father.

She understood him well, and she knew that under his dry exterior he was suffering deeply from remorse at the accident which had killed Dave Berry. But he was a stubborn man, and once set on a course, nothing could sway him from his purpose. He meant to recover that gold. It was not, she realized, the actual value of the shipment which was driving him, although in his present extended position it had been a crippling blow.

It was rather, she surmised, his need to reassert his leadership in the basin, the leadership which Claude Wolfson was already threatening.

Sitting there, she attempted to analyze her feelings toward Wolfson. His very self-assured charm was obvious. He was well read, far better educated than most of the men she had come in contact with. But it went deeper than that.

In her own way she was a rebel of sorts, chafing under the strict restraints with which her father had raised his motherless daughter, and the single fact that Wolfson had stood up to her father, had actually dared him to try to interfere in the western side of the basin, had aroused her attention and whetted her curiosity.

Their relationship had developed, not because it had really been pressed on either side, but more by default, since there was no other man in that part of the country who even challenged her interest.

If a showdown came—and she was certain that one was on the way, only delayed by the theft of this gold which had for days occupied her father's attention—she did not know on which side of the fence she would find herself.

And then, to complicate her thinking, she had run into Belmont in the hills. She had ridden out that morning with no purpose in view save to avoid meeting her father, for Ab Sellers had been furious when he learned of her part in securing the court order which had freed Belmont and the boy and that she had succeeded in taking him safely out of the country.

Remembering his words, she felt her cheeks redden in the darkness and knew a sense of shame that she had not considered the boy and what the events of the last few days had done to him.

She was conscious of having seen him only once in daylight, the morning on which his father had died, as he rode out of town, following his mother. She had not at the time been aware of who they were and had given them little thought, but now her memory traced back the picture—the gaunt woman on the ribby horse, the boy, too tall for his age, gawky, not properly developed or filled out.

She shivered a little. The woman was dead, and the boy hiding somewhere in the hills, and in this whole basin no one cared—no one but a drifter, a saddle tramp, a useless, anchorless individual whom she would probably not see again.

Instinctively her hand came up, and she wiped the back of it across her mouth in an effort to erase the memory of his unwanted kiss. But she knew, in some remote, detached way, that she would not soon forget him.

Yet, curiously, there was no clear picture of him in her mind. She had not been that interested. He was a rider, dressed no differently than a hundred horsemen she saw every day. She could not have told with full certainty what color his eyes were—blue or grey, she thought, but was not sure. He was tall, at least he had given that impression, walking at Claude Wolfson's side along the dark street, and his face had a peculiar hawk-like quality, perhaps because of its thinness.

She stirred and tried consciously to put the

thought of him away from her. Somehow it gave her a sense of unease, a sense that somehow she had failed in something which should have been done.

And then she saw the fat form of Honest John as he turned his horse into Stanton's main street and rode along it to the corner of the courthouse which held the sheriff's office.

There was a lamp burning in the office, and in the reflected glow from the window she saw the fat man lift himself heavily out of the saddle, tie the horse to the rail and cross to disappear into Glass' office.

She had no particular interest in him. She let her attention wander to three men who loitered before the saddle store, their bodies showing faintly in the half darkness, only the glowing coals of their cigarettes seeming to be alive and real, three punchers gossiping idly.

And then her attention came back to the courthouse door, for Glass's tall figure had appeared and he was hurrying across the dust ribbon of the street to disappear through the swinging doors of the Cattle Queen. He had hardly vanished before the doors again flapped open and he reappeared, followed this time by her father and two other men. They recrossed the street and entered the courthouse office, and now her sluggish interest was fully awake.

She sat for a moment, speculating on what might have occurred, and then she rose and with a purposeful step came down off the porch and crossed to the courthouse.

Inside the sheriff's office there were loud voices. She pressed open the door and stood there staring in at the smoky room. The fat man was the center of the group, and his voice was high with a kind of childish vindictiveness.

'I tell you he just shot Bronc Charley. All we were doing was trying to make the boy tell us where your gold is hidden, Mr. Sellers.'

Her father's voice was dry. 'And just why were you so interested, John?'

'Why,' said Honest John, and puffed his cheeks out in self-righteousness, 'we felt kind of responsible—Charley and me. We live in Toprock, and we've had trouble before and we didn't want you to get the idea that all of us up on the hill are bad.'

'I see.' Her father's tone was drier. There was no liking in his face for this fat man, no liking in any of their faces. Honest John stood alone and knew it, and he was a little helpless before this concentrated dislike, but he faced it down as he had faced down many things during his dubious career.

He said, 'Charley had his faults, but he was my friend and I hate to see him shot down in cold blood. Aren't any of you going after this drifter? He's a killer, I tell you—nothing but a cold-blooded killer.'

Helen Sellers saw that Glass was looking at her father as if for instructions, and she thought with a touch of disdain that this was the full story of Barney Glass's life, this always looking for instructions from someone else. He was a handsome man, a year or two older than she was. She had known him all her life, and there had been a time when she had thought that he might be the one.

That he still thought so and that he told her so every chance he got was one of the minor crosses of her life, and the fact that her father viewed him as an acceptable son-in-law had not made things easier.

She knew exactly why her father looked with favor on Barney Glass. Her father dominated him. Her father could not stand to have anyone around whom he did not dominate.

He was saying now, 'It's all right, John, and you can rest assured that we'll do something about it. And you can also be sure that if we find him and recover the gold you won't be forgotten.'

That was her father's way. Ab Sellers paid men for what he got. He never accepted a favor from anyone, especially anyone as low on the scale as Honest John was.

Helen heard her father say, 'Round up every man you can, Barney. We'll throw a net out through the hills that not even a snake could wiggle out of. We'll find this Belmont and the boy, and when we do we'll probably find the gold.'

103

She was in the room now, facing them. They were surprised to see her. They had been so intent on their discussion that they had not noticed her in the doorway.

'Wait a minute,' she said. She had not intended to speak so quickly, not in front of the other men or in front of Honest John. She did not like arguing with her father, certainly not in public.

She saw his small jaws tighten until his face looked dried, a trifle sunken. 'Keep out of this, girl.'

She said steadily, 'You aren't going to hunt this man down, to hound the boy.'

'He's a murderer.'

'How do you know that?' She was facing him now, for the other men in the room had stepped aside as if to be out of the line of fire. 'You have only his word for it.' She pointed a scornful finger at Honest John, who seemed to cringe beneath her contemptuous look. 'Would you take his word for anything—for anything?'

Her father was controlling himself with an obvious effort. 'This is your fault.' His voice had the dry sound of rustling leaves. 'If you hadn't talked that court order out of the judge, the man would be in jail and Bronc Charley still alive.'

She had an instant's wonder that she was no longer afraid of him. All of her childhood had been a time of wordless fear, that he might be offended by something which she said or did, that his dry, sarcastic voice might flay her with the biting quality of a multi-lashed whip.

But that fear was gone, and she faced him now, understanding him better than he understood himself, knowing that his ego was his weakness and that anything which deflated it struck at him deeply.

'What would have happened had he stayed in jail?' She was saying things in public which would better have been said in the privacy of their home, but she had to stop him now if he was to be stopped at all. 'Do you want another accidental hanging to rest heavy on your memory?'

His face greyed as her words struck home, and she saw him sway slightly, and had the sudden terrifying thought that he might be having a seizure.

She heard Barney Glass say gratingly, 'Helen, keep out of this. You've already done harm enough.'

She turned on the sheriff then, and her anger flashed into a live, burning thing. 'You,' she said, 'you are even more guilty than they are, a man sworn to uphold the law, a man who let a prisoner be taken from the safety of his cell with no attempt to halt them, with no move to arrest them afterward for what they did.'

He could not meet her stare. His brown eyes fell away to glare helplessly at a spot on

105

the floor between his booted feet.

But she was not finished with him yet. 'And now you and my father are pleased. You have another excuse to hunt a man down, a man whose only crime is that he and he alone chose to befriend a friendless boy. I'm ashamed of you. I'm ashamed of you both. If either of you rides out of this town on an errand of this kind I'll never speak to you again.'

She turned then and stormed out of the room, leaving behind her a blank silence which was heavier than any words. But she had no illusion that she had won. She knew her father too thoroughly for that. And she also knew the sheriff. Barney Glass had taken orders far too long. Whatever his personal feelings might have been, the habit of obedience was too strong. He would do exactly what Ab Sellers told him to.

11.

From her chair on the porch Helen Sellers watched the manhunt start, her white teeth drawing a tight line across her lower lip. She saw the sheriff move from one saloon to the next, calling the citizens of the town away from their nightly card games and drinking. She saw her father in the street, talking to a rider, and saw the rider start out for the Sellers' home ranch, and knew that before morning broke the dark of the night sky the full crew of the Box S would be in the saddle and joining the search.

She had no doubt but that other riders would head out to alert the other outfits of the eastern basin. Her father was not one to do things by halves, and his word was nearly law with most of the ranchers.

She wished there was some way she could warn Belmont and the boy—at least, she thought, they deserved some warning. She hoped that immediately after Bronc Charley's death they had mounted their horses and headed out of the country, but she doubted this.

Belmont, she supposed, would probably linger to recover the gold, for she had no faith that any man in his position would turn his back on such quick riches. And then something else occurred to her, just as Glass and his hastily-mustered posse rode out of town. She thought of Claude Wolfson.

Wolfson would not take kindly to the men from the basin's eastern edge riding out over his range, not even if they were a legally constituted posse, not even if they were hunting a murderer. And if they did not patrol the country behind Wolfson to the west, Belmont and the boy might well slip through the resulting hole.

The thought had hardly come before she acted upon it. She rose and went quickly into the lobby, mounting the stairs and moving along the upper hall to her room. Here she changed rapidly to riding garb, and ten minutes later was impatiently waiting in the runway of the livery while the puzzled barn man saddled her horse.

Riding out the west road she thought that certainly she was burning the last of her bridges behind her. She had known for months now that some day she and her father would have to come to a parting of the ways, but she had not expected it so soon, or thought that it would come in this manner.

And she also knew that by riding out here she was in a sense putting herself into Wolfson's power, since she was lining up with him against her father.

Carefully she considered Wolfson, knowing deep within her that she had decided some time back that she would finally many him. There was much that she liked about him, his looks, his drive and eagerness for success, the unfearing way that he had taken his stand against her father. And his humor, his ready ability to laugh at things—sardonically, yes, but still to laugh. This was something which her father had never learned.

Yet deep in the recesses of her mind there was still a reserve. There was, she realized, a certain unfeeling hardness about the man, a hardness which he kept well concealed so that it was hardly noticeable, yet present none the less.

She tried to justify it in her own mind, facing the fact that Wolfson had been forced to stand alone, that it had been necessary to bring in a fighting crew to hold his gains against the rest of the basin, but the nagging doubt lingered in her subconscious.

The sky was nearly fully light when she came to the mouth of the canyon and turned upward into the ranch yard. Smoke rose from the cookhouse chimney, and the ranch dog, a mongrel of startling yellow color, raced out, his yapping bringing men to the bunkhouse door. She ignored them and rode directly for the main house, seeing Claude Wolfson come out onto the porch to stare at her, as he ran his hand through his uncombed curly hair.

'Helen.' He wasted no time on useless greeting. 'What's happened?'

She swung from the saddle then and, dropping the trailing reins, mounted the single step to his side. Rapidly she told him what had occurred in town the night before, anger coming up into her eyes at the memory.

'They're out hunting him down like a dog,' she said. 'And his only crime was to befriend that boy.'

'I tried to get him to stay here.' Wolfson's voice was a murmur, but his eyes beneath the heavy brows had sharpened and he was

109

watching her intently without seeming to. 'He wouldn't listen. I don't think he's worth very much, a tramp.'

She said hotly, 'Is that any reason for him to die?'

Wolfson said evenly, 'He did shoot a man, you say.'

'A man?' she said. 'If he shot Charley he had good and sufficient cause. You certainly haven't a good word for Charley, have you?'

He shook his head. 'No, and not for John, either. This part of the world would be a better place if Toprock and all its citizens were cleaned out. But what's your interest?'

She flushed under the steady intentness of his gaze, then let her eyes fall as she said, 'No interest, except to see a little justice in this place. I got them out of jail to keep my father from making a further fool of himself, and then I met him on the rim . . .'

'You did not tell me that.'

'There was no reason to tell you.' Unaccountably, she was becoming angry. 'I met him by accident the morning he left your place.'

'He said he was leaving the country.' Wolfson's tone was colorless. 'Better for him if he had not changed his mind.'

'He was hunting the boy,' she explained. 'We only had a few words, but in those words he made me ashamed that I—that none of us had so much as given the boy a second's thought.'

Wolfson held his peace.

'He may be a drifter,' her tone showed that she was even ready to argue this, 'but at least he had a sympathetic feeling for the boy, a desire to help. A man should not be hunted down for that.'

'What is it you want me to do?'

She said, 'They'll come this way. They are starting a line at the south end of the basin and riding slowly north, a net to trap them if they try to get out that way, while others are riding to Toprock to pick up the trail. They're taking Indian George with them, and they'll be behind Belmont and the boy while the men from the south close in in front of them.'

'I see.'

She was disappointed in him, disappointed in the lack of interest he showed. She said, 'They'll be riding across your range. You don't want that, do you?'

'I don't want that,' he agreed.

'Then stop them. They'd hesitate to tangle with your crew. Stop them and turn them back. Tell them that you'll patrol this section if you must, but pass the word among your men to let Belmont and the boy escape.'

He seemed to be thinking, and her voice grew impatient. 'Well?'

'If that is what you want.' He said it slowly.

'That's what I want.'

'All right.' He had come to a decision. It

111

showed both in his tone and in the change in his manner. 'Now, you'd better get back to town. You wouldn't want to be here when they arrive.'

She knew that she had been dismissed, and it heightened her annoyance. Everything seemed to be wrong this morning. Claude might have at least offered her a cup of coffee. She had had no food since the night before.

She said, 'All right,' shortly, and turned away down the step to catch the trailing reins and swing up into the saddle.

Wolfson followed her. He said, 'Stop worrying. None of this is your fault.'

She did not answer directly. She merely said, 'Good-bye,' and swung the horse and spurred out of the yard, taking out her feeling of dissatisfaction on the animal.

Claude Wolfson watched her go. He was a man who seldom forgot an incident or a chance word, analyzing each through the ordered processes of his careful mind.

He sensed a change in Helen Sellers and found it not to his liking. He considered it carefully and by the time he had crossed the hard-baked surface of the yard and entered the cook shack he had come to his conclusion. The interest which she showed in this strange rider was a dangerous thing. He did not think that it had developed as yet to the point where it might cause him trouble, and he had no intention of letting it so develop. He had nothing against Belmont. In fact, in a half conscious way he was a little thankful to the man for having killed the blacksmith. Bronc Charley had been the most dangerous of the Toprock people, and he had known for some time that he must clean them out.

But he could not have Helen Sellers giving her attention to anyone else. He had planned too carefully for that. Some day, through this girl, he meant to take over the whole basin. Not that he did not love her. He loved her, he realized, as much as he was capable of ever loving anyone, but his love was tempered by other considerations.

He ate in silence, ignoring the crew as they straggled in and sat silently for their breakfast. He knew that they had seen the girl ride up and that they were curious, but he gave no indication of this knowledge until the last man had finished and shoved back his empty plate.

Then Wolfson said, 'You remember the drifter who was here yesterday?'

They looked up, showing little enthusiasm.

'He murdered a man at Toprock,' Wolfson said. 'The sheriff has alerted the whole basin. There will be men riding through here sometime today. For reasons of my own I don't want outsiders on my range.'

They watched him now, their attention growing. There was an explosive quality about this group of men, lurking behind the quiet mask of their bearded faces. They had been in

113

trouble most of their lives, until it had become a habit which was hard to shake. The steady, everyday drudgery of the ranch routine palled upon them, and they had grown restless and sullen with its boredom. But now they sensed the chance for a fight.

He said, 'We don't want trouble with the sheriff's men, if we can avoid it.' This last he emphasized. The time had come, he felt, to show his strength, to make the men of the eastern basin realize that he was a power who had to be considered, who could no longer be ignored. And this was as good a time as any, when at least a portion of their concentration was diverted to the manhunt.

'You mean you want to see this drifter get away?' It was Doane, his riding boss, who asked the question.

He shook his head. 'I don't want him to get away, but I don't want outsiders on our range either. Is that clear?'

They considered his words, turning and twisting them in their narrow minds, trying, he supposed, to find his reason, and not finding it. But he did not care.

One thing he was certain of—no matter what happened they would not talk. There was no mixing between his crew and the rest of the riders who worked within the basin. They were a group apart.

'You know,' he said, 'that ten thousand dollars in gold was stolen from the stage and hidden somewhere in the hills.'

Their interest was sharper now. It was as if he had thrown a bone to a pack of hungry dogs.

'This drifter is supposed to know where it's hidden. If you run into him in the hills you could ask him if you wish and, if afterward he could not talk, the gold would belong to the man who located it.' He rose then and quietly left the room.

Behind him there was no sudden burst of conversation. Each man was buried in his own thoughts, already daydreaming of the many pleasing ways in which that gold could be spent.

Wolfson smiled darkly to himself, knowing that by his talk he had set up two things. First, his full crew would see that no sheriff's man invaded their range. They would want no competition in their hunt for Belmont. And second, Belmont, if located on the west side of the basin, had very small chance to survive. However, Wolfson was only partly content.

Three things could happen. Belmont and the boy might succeed in making good their escape. If that happened, so be it, for Belmont would not be apt to ride this way again and, although Helen might remember him with a certain curiosity, that curiosity would offer little threat to Wolfson's plans. Or Belmont might run into some of the ranch crew. That also would be a final end, and his body would likely never be found in the hills.

The one real danger was that the sheriff's posse might catch up with him, for in that case they would most certainly try to take him alive, since a dead man could not tell them what Sellers wished to know.

In that event he would probably be brought back to town and locked in jail, and possibly be tried for Charley's murder. At the thought, Wolfson's mouth corners drew down. That, from his point of view, would be the worst of all, for it would mean that the girl would see Belmont again and have her already aroused sympathy heightened by his plight. Then he undoubtedly would become a martyr in her eyes.

Basically, Wolfson had a poor opinion of women. He felt that too often they were ruled by their emotions rather than their common sense, and even though he loved her he still felt that Helen Sellers shared this weakness.

He wished that somehow he could assure Belmont's capture by his own crew. He was even tempted to ride with some of them to Toprock in an effort to pick up the hunted man's trail. But he discarded the idea almost as soon as it formed in his mind.

Somehow, Helen Sellers would hear of his action and the very purpose he was striving for would be defeated. Also, the sheriff's men were well ahead of him. They would already

116

be following the twisting trail. All he could do now was wait and hope. Slowly he mounted to the porch and went into the house.

12.

The men of Wolfson's crew gathered in a tight group beside the corral fence, unconscious that Wolfson watched them through the ranch house window, and they discussed what he had told them that morning.

There was not one of them who showed any shock at the proposal, or any sympathy for Belmont or the boy. Long years of near banditry had squeezed out of them the softer emotions, leaving little save a coating of cynical, jeering amusement with which they faced the world. This mockery was in itself a sham, since there was far more cruelty than humor, a front which weak men used to gloss over their own inner fears.

Doane was a big man with a broken nose and a knife scar under his right eye, mementos of some forgotten barroom fight. Of them all, he came closest to being an experienced cattleman, although that experience had been gained mostly with stolen herds.

He said now in his heavy voice, 'Let's study this thing. First, the boss wants this drifter killed. I don't know why, but I can guess.' He leered a little then, and the men before him exchanged their knowing looks. There was not one of them who had not commented on Helen Sellers' visits to the ranch.

'Who cares?' Ben August said, spitting through his broken teeth.

Doane looked at him, and the movement of his thick shoulders was more expressive than any words. He said, 'The point is, we want that gold. I don't like the way things are building up here, and a man gets thin fighting for forty per and found, but unless this Belmont gets across Black Canyon we'll never find him on this side of the range. He'll head back north or try to cut east of the basin, and either way the sheriff's men will ride him down without our ever seeing him.'

They thought about it and failed to like the thought, their faces turning flat and masklike with their disappointment.

Doane said, 'But there is one way across Black Canyon, and maybe the kid with him knows it and will show him, an old deer trail that climbs this side. I used it once.'

They were listening now, intently.

'It comes up through a narrow side canyon. Three or four men could be waiting when he got to the top, and we might have a chance to grab him alive. Wolfson may want Belmont dead, but a dead man isn't going to show us where that gold is cached.'

Their eyes had brightened now, refreshed

118

by avarice and growing hope.

'Some of us will have to stay here,' he added. 'Wolfson will want us to the south to warn the sheriff's men off the range, and we want them warned. If we get the gold we want a clear road out of this country.'

They looked at each other.

'Four should be enough at the canyon. I'll have to go because I am the only one who knows the place, but the rest of you can draw straws to decide. Those of us who go will promise to meet the others if we get the gold. We'll have to come south, so there won't be too much chance of a double-cross.'

They considered that also, glancing sidewise at the men about them. There was little trust among them.

Doane ignored this. He straightened and walked over to a clump of grass and broke the dry stems, snapping three off to less than two inches long, the rest longer. Then he came back to the fence with the straws gripped between his broad thumb and finger, the lower half of the straws concealed by his cupped palm.

Silently he moved about the rough circle, offering a straw to each man. The three with the short stalks would ride with him. Ben August was the first to draw, and he drew a short one. He looked at it, not certain that he was happy with his luck. August was not a man with much bravery, or one who enjoyed a

119

fight. He would not have been working for Wolfson at all except for Doane, for in a sense he was little more than Doane's shadow, having no will power or decision of his own.

Bob DeVoto and a man known only as Cinder drew the other short straws, both hardened ruffians, handy with their guns, and lacking entirely in conscience of any kind. Doane was satisfied. If he had been taking his pick he would have chosen these men.

'Get your horses,' he told them. 'The rest of you go up to the house for riding orders. If Wolfson asks where we've gone, tell him that I have an idea that he may see Belmont dead before the sun goes down.'

*   *   *

At almost the same time that they were saddling their mounts, Ross Belmont was building up the fire in Black Canyon. As he straightened from gathering an arm load of wood, he heard a horse coming, and dropped the sticks, standing motionless in the sheltering brush, his hand on his gun.

He did not relax until he recognized Mary Lu as she rode into sight, a bulky parcel tied behind her saddle, but he forgot his hunger at her first words.

'You've got to get out of here. They're hunting you. They want you for murder.'

He stared at her. 'Murder?'

120

'Bronc Charley,' she said, slipping from the saddle. 'John went into the sheriff's office. He told Sellers and Glass that he saw the fight. He claimed that Charley wasn't even wearing a gun. He says you shot him in cold blood.'

The girl's excited voice had roused the boy. He sat up, rubbing the sleep from his heavy eyes, then rose to stand at Belmont's side.

Belmont was staring at the girl as if he did not quite believe what she said, as if he were trying to read a second meaning into her words. She sensed this. Long training had hardened her to the knowledge that many people lied, and that both her motives and statements were often open to question.

She said with a touch of rebellion in her tone, 'You don't believe me, but it's the truth.'

Belmont said slowly, 'Why would John do a thing like that? He's no friend of Sellers'. What does he stand to gain?'

She shook her head. 'He's just mad, I guess. And Bronc Charley was his friend—about the only friend he ever had. And maybe he's afraid of you. Maybe he thinks that if they kill you or capture you he might still stand a chance at questioning Davey.'

'How do you know all this?'

She said, 'The sheriff and some men are already at Toprock. I heard them talking. They routed out everyone and questioned them, and they brought Bronc Charley's body in.'

He was convinced.

'They're only waiting for daylight,' she told him. 'They have an Indian trailer with them. You've got to move.'

He nodded and without a word turned downward toward the horses. They had to get out of this canyon. He knew that. It was a good hiding place, but it was also a trap. When he came back leading the animals, the girl silently handed him some cold meat and dry biscuits. The boy was already eating.

Belmont stuffed the food into his pocket. He used his hat to bring water from the creek to douse the fire. The embers steamed and died, but he knew that the odor of the smoke would linger in the air, that the odor might well lead the pursuit to this canyon even if Glass' men failed to find their tracks.

But even as he turned again to the horses his mind was busy weighing possibilities, and before he mounted he said to the girl, 'Maybe it would be the smart thing to give myself up.'

She stared at him as if he had taken leave of his senses. 'Give yourself up? They'll hang you.'

He said, 'You were a witness. John hasn't considered that. He doesn't know that you were anywhere near.'

The boy said sharply, insistently, 'Remember what happened to my dad.'

Belmont was remembering.

'Who'd believe me?' The girl's tone was

deep with bitterness. 'I'm from Toprock. Even if Davey went in they still would not believe the both of us, because they don't want to.'

The man said, 'If Davey told them where the gold was . . .' and let the words hang between them in the chill morning air.

The boy looked at him, but did not answer. The thin face was a set mask, and he thought with climbing anger—the young fool would rather see us both hang than give Sellers his gold. I should have ridden away yesterday. I should ride away now and leave them here, because if Glass' men locate the boy they'll waste little time on me.

But he knew that he was not going to, that something he did not quite understand would keep him from doing so.

He said to the boy, 'Know the way out of this trap?'

The girl spoke quickly, 'I'll show you.'

His tone was rougher than he intended. 'You're going back to Toprock and stay there. You're mixed up in this enough.'

Her face got a stubborn look which wiped its small prettiness away and somehow reminded him of the boy. She said, 'I'm going with you. Davey's the only friend I ever had.'

He considered. He knew that this was not the time for argument, that they had to get out of this canyon quickly.

'All right, then.' He was in the saddle, watching her mount, seeing her turn upstream between the narrow canyon walls. He saw the boy fall in behind her, and then followed as they picked their way along the bank of the rushing water.

This was the way they had to go, and yet, had he been alone, not knowing the country, he would not have dared to chance it, for the canyon might well be a box, its sides and end too steep for a horse to climb. And they had to keep their horses. Without them they would stand no chance at all.

The timber was becoming more dense now, and at times the aspen were so close together that it was difficult for the horses to force their way through. He was glad of the cover, since it would prevent anyone from seeing them from the rim above. But he watched the canyon walls with a nagging worry as they showed no sign of leveling. In fact, if anything they seemed steeper as the twisting turns led them back deeper into the rising hills.

The sun had now reached a height that allowed its rays to clear the eastern rim and strike downward to the rushing river below. This brought a certain warmth, and Belmont welcomed it. Now at least there was no danger that the noise of their progress would be heard by anyone. The rattling, gurgling roar of the creek drowned all other sound.

And the girl never hesitated, never slackened her pace, never paused in uncertainty. Either she had been this way before, or she lacked the brains to realize that they might be working deeper and deeper into a trap.

And then they reached it—a deer trail which slanted up the western wall, a faint trace, hardly a trail at all and one which Belmont would never have seen in the screen of heavy brush.

She dismounted then and motioned them to get down, and pulled some food from her saddlebag and began to eat, silently, deliberately, with all the single-minded intentness of an animal.

Belmont followed suit. The meat, venison he judged, was tough and stringy, dry. The biscuits were hard, not risen properly and tasting a little of raw flour. But it was food, and he chewed doggedly, and afterward had his drink from the rushing creek, the water so chill that it stung his teeth.

He wanted a smoke, wanted it as badly as he had ever craved tobacco in his life, but forced the thought from his mind, turning to look at the girl and then at the faint line of the trail climbing upward.

'You ever been up that?'

She nodded, and he was forced to believe her. 'With a horse?'

Again she nodded and, as if to prove her point, turned into the track and began to climb, leading her unwilling mount. The boy went next and finally Belmont.

The rise of the grade was sharp. At places he was thankful for the thick growth, for he seemed to actually pull himself up by grasping one tree and then the next, tugging the reluctant horse until it followed. Twice the animal slipped and then, snorting, plunged ahead in an effort to find firmer footing. Both times Belmont was forced to jump aside to keep from being trampled.

Never afterward did he remember exactly how long the climb took. The trail wound and twisted, following the contours of the ground. At some points it leveled off, running along the canyon wall, at others it dipped downhill, climbing again when it found a crevice up which it could make its tortuous way.

Two-thirds of the distance up, they reached a mounded hogback behind which there was a depression nearly as large as a small-sized room. Here on the comparatively level ground the girl halted, waiting for her companions to catch up with her. The boy, used to the thinness of the mountain air, showed little visible effect from the climb.

Belmont's lungs ached, and his heart felt as if it were too large for his body. He breathed noisily through his mouth, gulping air in a desperate effort to absorb sufficient oxygen. His knees had a weak, rubbery feel, and his skin felt flushed with a slight burning sensation.

The girl, observing him, said, 'The rest is

easier and we haven't too far to go.'

He looked upward. They had left the aspen and were in pine, slim trees which grew to sixty or seventy feet, so closely bunched that their lower branches had rotted away, leaving trunks as bare as if they had been limbed by man. The timber hid the crest and also hid the sight of the canyon below them. It was as if they were anchored in a small island, lost in a dark green sea.

Faintly from below came the roar of the hurrying water, faintly from above the breath of wind, swaying the treetops at the canyon's rim. But here was quiet, and peace, and there was enough break in the foliage above the hogback to allow a spray of sunshine to trickle through.

Belmont looked below them, thankful for the trees. Without them they would not have been able to climb this wall, and he knew now that there had been small chance of falling. Neither a man nor a horse could have gone far down that slope without coming up hard against a fence of trunks.

They moved on, the girl still in the lead, and, true to her promise, the going was easier, the canyon wall shelved into a more gentle slope, and the track was wider and better marked.

Belmont wondered by what series of accidents the first deer had come this way. For there must have been a first, a pioneer in whose prints other animals had followed. He looked upward and saw that they were coming to the top. Here the lip of the rim was lower than to the right or left, for the trail ran up into a shallow side canyon that at some forgotten time must have carried a small stream of water.

The girl ahead had stopped and was mounting, and thankfully Belmont lifted his own body into the saddle. His knees felt spongy, and his lungs seemed to have a tight iron band about them which prevented him from getting enough air.

He did not know how far they had climbed, but at a guess he would have said that it was well over a thousand feet. Looking back, he could see little save the trunks of the trees through which they had passed.

The girl and Davey halted and he rode up to them, saying, 'Where do we go from here?'

With one hand she made a circle toward the west. 'You'll have to get over that range or cut back down through the basin.'

Ross Belmont stared at the distant range showing faintly above the treetops, its sheer, bare peaks still clothed in the heavy snow blanket which the season's sun had not yet melted. They looked very high, very solid and unbroken, and he shivered a little at the thought.

He knew little about the country to the west, but enough to know that it was bleak and barren and sparsely populated. It did not enter his mind to question the girl's statement. By showing him the deer trail, she had proved that she knew far more about the area than he did, but he still felt that this was not the place for her and told her so, suggesting that since they were now clear of the canyon she ride back to Toprock, saying it was foolish to think of going on.

She did not argue. In fact, she did not trouble to answer. Instead, she swung her horse and rode on up through the timber of the side canyon, not even looking back to make sure they followed.

She was still ahead and almost at the crest when the rifle shot slammed out of the brush. It was so utterly unexpected that for an instant Ross Belmont was too surprised even to react.

All the way along the stream and during the climb up the canyon side he had had a sense of flight, a feeling that they might be closely pursued. But with the width of the canyon between him and Toprock he had unconsciously relaxed.

His surprise lasted for an instant only, for he saw the girl's horse rear, and realized that it had been hit, and saw her fighting it, and then saw her kick free of the stirrups and half slide, half fall from her mount as it twisted and, taking a dozen steps, dropped. She fell on her knees and at once scrambled upright with a lightness which told him she was not hurt.

The boy had pulled to one side and hauled up, tugging his rifle from its place beneath his leg, and Belmont shouted at him as he raced past, 'Go on, get out of sight.'

Then he forgot the boy. Kicking his foot out of the near stirrup and checking his horse, he caught Mary Lu under the arms, swinging her up to a place behind the saddle and, pivoting the horse in a single motion, he sent it headlong into the shelter of the brush which grew thickly on the sloping canyon side. As he drove forward, the rifle cracked again and a bullet clipped a small branch inches from his ear.

He heard a crashing on his left and knew it was the boy and angled over until he could see him. The boy had his rifle free across the bow of the saddle. His face showed white, and there was a pinched, startled look about his eyes.

Belmont motioned to him with his free hand to halt, and hauled up himself. They sat in silence, nothing breaking the stillness for the moment but the heaviness of their breathing.

Then, somewhere behind them, a voice called through the timber. 'Work them south. Don't let them circle back. Hold them against the canyon rim.'

Afterward there was the movement of horses, unseen in the heavy timber, then the voice again. 'Belmont! Belmont! We've got you. Throw down your gun and come out—walking, with your hands up. You won't be hurt. All we want is the gold.'

The girl was sitting behind him, her arms tight about his stomach. They contracted a little more, and her lips were close to his ear as she whispered, 'They were waiting for us at the head of the trail.'

He had already figured that out for himself. It was so obvious that anyone should have expected it. For one bare moment he thought she had purposely played them false, then he realized that this was absurd. But how had they known?

She was still whispering, 'It can't be any of the sheriff's men from Toprock. They couldn't get across the canyon. They would have to go around from the south or follow us. There's no other way across.'

At the instant he did not care who they were, but he did wonder how many, and how closely they were ringed about him. Had he been alone he would have taken a chance on trying to break through, but with the boy and girl to think of it was a different problem.

The land around them was very rough and heavily timbered. Rock masses jutted up in irregular formations, some solid and unfractured, others shattered into piles of broken stone. He pulled behind the nearest of these, the boy following, and swung his right leg up and over the horse's neck so that he slid to the ground without disturbing the girl from her place behind the saddle.

He reached up then and snaked his rifle from its boot and stepped away, looking upward into their worried eyes.

'Drift back into the timber.' It was an order. 'I'll center their attention on these rocks, and when they start to close in you ride around them.'

Mary Lu stared down at him with eyes which seemed much too large for her small, white face. 'But you . . . ?'

His whisper was harsh. 'Do as I say. They really want the kid, not me. When they find he's gone I'll be all right.'

He did not actually believe this last, but he had to say something. He had to get them out of here, and he was counting on Mary Lu's worry about the boy. He saw her glance in the kid's direction and knew he had used the right argument.

Her feeling for this boy was the strongest emotion of her life. He saw her reach forward and put one hand on the horn, the other on the cantle, and hunch her slight body forward into the deep seat. Then she raised her hand and swung the horse easily away, the boy after a brief hesitation following. She rode like a man, and he judged that most of her waking hours had been spent in the saddle.

But he forgot her almost at once,

scrambling up the rock pile which rose a good fifty feet above the pine-needled carpet of the ground, hunting until he found a sheltered place near the top. Then he sent a ringing challenge through the trees.

'Come and get me!'

13.

Had Doane been more familiar with the country, he and his men would have reached the ambush before Belmont topped out of the canyon, but he overshot his mark and was forced to retrace his slow way back along the canyon rim, so that they had barely found the trail when the mounted girl appeared suddenly from the trees ahead.

Ben August was the one who shot her horse. Ben was as jittery as usual and Doane, riding at his side, turned to curse him, thus blocking the men behind for the precious seconds it took Belmont to swing her up behind his saddle and dash into the sheltering brush.

Doane cursed him savagely. 'You fool. Belmont's no good to us dead. We want him alive.' He swung, motioning Cinder and Bob DeVoto south to head off the fugitives against the brink of the canyon rim, then he raised his voice, calling Belmont's name, telling him that he would not be hurt if he surrendered.

He got no answer and swung to Ben August. 'They're in there somewhere. You ride ahead, I'll follow and flush them.'

August stared at the fence of trees, remembering something Doane either ignored or had forgotten. Belmont was armed, and Belmont had no reason to hold his fire, no reason to wish to keep them alive.

When Belmont shouted, it startled August so that he nearly fell from his horse.

His impulse was to turn and ride away, but he knew that if he did and Doane discovered it he was as good as dead. For he feared Doane with a kind of fascination which would not let him break away. Their paths had joined some half dozen years before, and they had ridden together along a dozen shady trails which had caromed them from the Kansas frontier clear down through the dry, burning sands of the southwest.

He pulled his horse around, riding forward cautiously, hearing Doane somewhere on his left, hearing the muffled curses of Cinder and Bob DeVoto to the right.

So they converged on the rock pile, having no difficulty finding it, since Belmont's voice kept taunting them. It was as if he had lost his senses, as if he had eaten locoweed. He kept howling like an irritated Apache, mocking them from the nest he had found among the tumbled boulders, the split, jagged pieces of granite.

Had any of them been thinking with clarity they must have guessed that there was a method in his shouting, but at the moment they were riding in for the kill, driven by the urgent excitement of the manhunt, sparked on by their desire for the gold.

Belmont, for all his shouting, was sharply alert. His main purpose was to attract and hold their attention, to hold it as long as he possibly could, giving the girl and the kid their chance to work around the men.

He had no idea how many they were, but he meant to center as much of their attention on himself as possible. He saw Ben August first, merely a glimpse of movement in the heavy brush, and raised his rifle and deliberately sent his shot crashing above August's head, and saw the man fade quickly back into the timber, and heard a yell from another direction.

'Belmont!'

He kicked another cartridge into the chamber and grinned faintly to himself. At least he knew where two of the men were.

'I can't hear you.'

Doane called back, 'You can hear all right, and you'd better listen to me. We're not the sheriff's men. We're Wolfson's crew.'

He heard that plainly enough, and the words brought a frown to shadow his eyes. Wolfson's crew. That explained some things—

how they had managed to be on the west side of the canyon—but it did not explain why they were taking a hand in this game.

He said loudly, 'All right. Tell Wolfson to step out. I owe him something for the other night.'

'He isn't here.'

Belmont had not made the mistake of letting his full attention center on Doane. He watched his rear also and now caught movement in the brush behind the rock pile, and judged that he was surrounded and grinned tightly.

At least the boy and girl had apparently eluded the circle, and once free in the brush they would be as hard to find as half-grown quail.

For himself he was not too worried at the moment. It would depend on how many were in the attacking party and on their willingness to rush him. He was fairly well protected; he had his rifle and his single-action Colts, and it was nearly fifty feet from the ground level to his perch. He did not believe that anyone could climb fast enough to reach him before he could shoot him from the rocks.

He said, 'If Wolfson isn't here, who's in command?'

'I am.' It was Doane. Now that he felt his quarry was cornered he dismounted, working forward from tree to tree until he could gain a full view of the rocks. 'We have nothing against you, Belmont.'

Ross Belmont chuckled without mirth and raised his voice again. 'I'd never have guessed it from the way you're acting.'

'All we want is a part of the gold. You'll never get it out of this country by yourself.'

For an instant of bitterness Ross Belmont thought how much trouble that gold had caused, and under his breath he cursed Davey for not telling where it was. The boy's stubbornness would get them all killed before this was finished. He stared downward at the circling trees, and his anger, which had risen against the boy, transferred itself to the men below.

At least the men riding with the sheriff were in effect following the dictates of the law, but these killers who had tracked him down had no interest in anything save the gold. He was not foolish enough to think that they would actually let him go, even if he turned the gold over to them. All this talk was merely an attempt to drag him into the open, to get him to tell them where Dave Berry had hidden his loot. He of course had no intention of coming out.

His one problem was water, but it was not hot on the high canyon rim, and he felt certain he could last through until evening. Once it was dark they could slip up on him, but also he would have an equal chance to slip away, and he had one advantage which they did not have. He was alone. Any movement in the darkness would be that of a foe. The hand he held was far from hopeless, and he had emerged from too many tight spots to give up easily.

He did not answer and Doane's patience slipped. It had seemed to him for one long moment that things were in their hands, that they had their victim cornered, and that he could not escape, but now it seemed to be something of a standoff. And then he realized that he had heard no word from the boy or from the girl who had had the horse shot from under her. Were they up on the rocks with Belmont or had they slipped away, perhaps to go after the gold?

He studied the rock pile from his tree shelter, knowing that the next move was up to him. But what to do? A chance bullet, ricocheting to strike Belmont's head, would make it impossible for him to tell them what they wished to know.

And then the decision was taken out of his hands, for as he shifted his position for a better look, a rifle cracked somewhere in the brush at his rear and a bullet tore directly past his ear to strike the tree behind which he hid.

For an instant he thought that one of his own followers had gotten behind him and shot at him by accident, and then he realized that this could not be so, that this had to be an attack by the boy. It could not conceivably be anyone else, and he cursed himself even as he turned, seeking cover by dropping beside a small rise of rock, shouting to Ben August and Cinder and DeVoto to watch themselves.

'The kid is loose somewhere in the timber!'

Belmont heard the yell and understood the words and swore under his breath. If Davey had only stayed out of sight, if Davey had only waited until night. He shifted, and his movement brought a shot from Cinder, who was to the south of his hiding place.

He saw the faint glow of the rimfire under the shadow of the trees and raised his rifle and sent his shot in return, aiming to the right of the flash as he faced it, and heard the thudding slap as the heavy ball found its mark, and the high, wild yell as the man died.

He had half risen to make his shot, and he drew fire from the three remaining Wolfson men. DeVoto's shot missed Belmont entirely, but Ben August put a neat hole through his hat. Only Doane's bullet found its mark, and this was nearly a miss, since the bullet tore through the space between Belmont's left arm and side, scraping a groove through the swell of the upper arm without touching the bone.

Doane paid for that shot with his life, for as he raised up to make it, Davey Berry, standing twenty yards away, put a bullet into the center of his back. He straightened, stumbled twice and then plunged rather than ran into the clear space below the rock pile, and fell headlong to earth in full sight of both Belmont and Ben August.

The sight was too much for August, already so nervous that he found it difficult to stay in a hiding place. He sent a high cry out for Cinder and got no response, and then yelled DeVoto's name. When he got a grumbling reply he almost shrieked, 'I'm pulling out!' He turned then, crashing back through the timber without regard for the noise he made, racing for his horse.

Ross Belmont heard him and made no effort to fire. DeVoto heard him and hesitated for an instant, then silently came about and followed, running to where his own horse was tethered.

Only Davey Berry moved, sifting through the trees in time to see Ben August mount, in time to send a bullet high over his head to speed him in his flight. Then the boy came back, moving as silently as a young deer through the trees, to find that Belmont had dropped down the rocks and worked quickly into the timber.

'They're gone. Rode out north.'

Belmont stared at him, at the young, thin face, at the hard eyes which met his unflinchingly. 'Sure of that?'

The boy nodded. 'There were only four.'

Belmont did not speak. He turned and moved over to examine Doane. The man was dead. So was Cinder, when they found him in

140

the far brush.

He straightened again, looking at the boy. 'Why did you have to creep back? I told you to get away.'

Davey Berry stared at him, and his small mouth set in a thin-lipped, solid line, but Belmont noticed that his chin trembled. 'I . . . I . . . I couldn't leave you.'

Belmont was surprised. He started to say something, flushed, and instead changed the subject. 'Where's Mary Lu?'

'She went back to Toprock.'

'Went back to Toprock?'

'Yes, sir.'

It was, Belmont thought, probably the only time the boy had ever called anyone sir in his life.

'The food she brought—it wasn't much— was on her horse when it got killed. We sneaked back there. The sack busted and the coffee was scattered on the ground, so was the beans and flour. She went to get more.'

Belmont shook his head slowly. 'How did she figure to get there safe?'

The boy smiled wisely. 'She can climb down a canyon wall where a horse couldn't go. There ain't no place Mary Lu can't go if she sets her mind.'

The man looked at him, a little dazed. These two children seemed to wander about that country at will, and some kind of providence seemed to watch over them. He said, 'If she went after more supplies she must be planning on coming back.'

'Not here,' Davey told him. 'She's going to meet us up at the Devil's Needle sometime tonight. Then we'll all get out of the country.'

Belmont had no idea where the Devil's Needle was. His single idea was to get himself and the boy out of the territory as quickly as they could, but looking at the distant snow-capped hills he knew that they would need food—yes, and luck, if they were to make it safely.

14.

The Sheriff's posse found where Belmont and the boy had camped at the bottom of Black Canyon. They found the camp ground about eleven and were puzzled as they located the three sets of tracks which led away up-canyon, having not the slightest idea who the third rider could be.

Barney Glass was in a bad humor. It had taken the Indian tracker much longer than he thought it should to find the camp. They had picked up the sign beside Bronc Charley's body, and trailed it through the rough country to the canyon's edge and down into bottom of the canyon itself.

Glass was not familiar with this country to

the west of Toprock. It was too rough for cattle and he had never been through it, nor did he have too much faith in Indian George.

The man was a half-breed—a plains Indian who had somehow drifted down here and gone to work on Sellers' ranch, a man of middle age who seldom spoke.

Glass had no faith in Indians of any kind and, until they found the charred remains of the small fire, he had been almost certain that the Indian was purposely leading them astray for some untold reason of his own.

He looked at George now, at the hawkish face, at the dark hair which fell to a straggling edge beneath the brim of the broken hat, and wrinkled his nose at the bathless smell which clung about him like an unpleasant aura.

'Which way?'

The half-breed studied the ground, going a little way up the canyon, and came back, pointing wordlessly.

They reached the deer trail finally and stared at it and then at the towering slope above. They needed no one to tell them that the fugitives had gone that way, but there was not a man among them who relished the thought of following.

And then, from far above them, the faint echoes of gunfire filled the canyon, and they climbed, spurred onward by recurrence of the firing above. But by the time they reached the top they found nothing except the girl's dead horse, two live ones tethered in the brush and two dead men.

The sheriff peered down at Doane's still body and recalled him from a single trip the man had made to town. He said to one of the riders beside him, 'That's one of Wolfson's men. I wonder what they were doing here. Wolfson was a friend of this Belmont man—at least he got him out of jail.'

The rider did not answer. The girl's dead horse surrounded by the scattered beans and coffee and flour, and the positions of the bodies, separated as they were by the upthrust of rock, offered a mystery which was not simple to read.

The Indian was circling through the brush, his quick, dark eyes reading the sign and translating it to his knowing brain. He found the woman's boot tracks, and the boy's, and saw the way they diverged and followed hers back to the canyon's edge, and noted the marks she left as she started the descent.

But he did not mention this to the sheriff. He came back, tracing the boy's tracks as Davey had circled behind the men, and found the empty shells the boy had spilled when he shot at Doane, and read the sign of the two men who had ridden away. Then he came again to Glass, making a sweeping gesture with a dirty hand.

They followed him, out along the trail Belmont and Davey had made as they headed

144

westward toward the snowy peaks, a good hour behind their prey. It was a wild land, imposing in the grandeur of its very roughness, cut up by washes and narrow gullies, studded with rock formations which jutted through the blanketing needles of the sheltering pines.

As they progressed the Indian felt a growing respect for the man he followed, for Belmont and his companion were taking advantage of every piece of stony ground, of every water course, of each chance to blot their tracks; but his mind kept reverting to the sign of a woman's boots which had led over the canyon rim, and he wondered who she was and what she had been doing with the hunted man.

*   *   *

As the sheriff and his posse reached the first rising grade which led toward the snowy peaks above, Helen Sellers was riding into Toprock.

Why she came she was not entirely sure. It was a portion of the basin of which she knew very little. After her return from the Wolfson ranch to find Stanton drained of men, she had spent two restless hours at the hotel, then, not able to contain herself longer, she had gone back to the livery stable, had a fresh horse saddled and set out on the four miles to the mountain hamlet.

145

She checked her horse at the foot of the irregular, grass-grown street, and sat gazing at the scattered cabins, feeling that she had been a fool to come here. The hunt undoubtedly had moved on, for it was hours since Glass and his men had taken the trail north, and there was probably no one in the town who could tell her more than she already knew.

But the feeling of guilty unease which had been riding her was more intense, and she started along the street slowly, seeing no one, yet having the feeling that she was being watched by unseen eyes.

She saw no one as she halted before the store building and sat for a long moment, wondering what she should do next; then the sound of angry voices came to her from the rear, and she put her horse around the building's corner, riding down the length of the log wall.

Honest John was there, his face red and balloon-like with rage, his fat hands clutching the arm of a slight girl who was trying to free herself. 'You thieving slut! I caught you finally.' There was a burlap sack on the ground beside them, fallen to its side, its mouth gaping open to expose its contents.

The girl made no sound, though the expression on her face showed the pain which John's grip brought to her.

'I caught you, and you're going to the sheriff . . .' John was puffing now. 'What did

146

you want with all them things? What . . .' Suddenly he jerked her toward him. 'Hey! You're a friend of Dave Berry's kid. I'll bet you was getting stuff for him and for that drifter.' He twisted her arm forcing her to her knees so that the dark, unruly hair fell like a curtain across her small, thin face. 'Where are they? Come on, talk up before I break your arm.'

'That will be enough.' Helen Sellers forced her horse forward until its nose almost touched the fat man's back. 'You hear me. Let her go.'

The fat man twisted his head around without releasing his grip on the girl's arm, snarling up at her. 'You keep out of this, you . . .' He stopped, his whole face sagging with surprise when he realized who it was.

'Miss Sellers . . .'

'Let her go.' Helen Sellers' voice was almost expressionless, and she flicked the quirt which dangled from its wrist loop suggestively.

'But . . .'

'Let her go.'

Reluctantly the fat man relinquished his grip on the girl's arm, but not before he gave it a final twist which brought a subdued cry of pain from her tight pressed lips.

The quirt flicked out like the tongue of a striking snake, the tiny metal collar at its end cutting the skin of the fat cheek so that blood flowed. Honest John howled, throwing up a protective arm and backing a few safe steps away.

'You shouldn't ought to have done that.'

Helen Sellers was suddenly raging at him. 'You fool! You're lucky I didn't get your eye.' She stared at him with contempt, feeling all the dislike she had experienced when he had come in with his tale to the sheriff's office. 'By rights I should have you driven out of the country.'

He gaped at her, his face a sagging yellow against which the small spot of blood showed extra red. 'I was just trying to help.'

'Like a coyote helps,' she said. 'How much are those things worth?' She pointed with the whip to the burlap sack.

John wet his lips. 'It ain't the worth,' he sounded as if he were near tears. 'It's that she's a thief, and stealing for them outlaws, and . . .'

'How much?'

He stared up into her hard eyes and let his own drop. 'Say ten dollars.'

'Put it on my account.' Helen Sellers had never carried money with her at any time while she was in the basin, and it did not occur to her that the powerful Box S ranch had no account with this mountain store.

Honest John gulped. He was caught in the middle and knew it. He had no love for the Sellerses, or for that matter for any of the

148

basin ranchers. His life had been spent in buying stolen beef and anything else that the people around him could pilfer from the big landholders. Yet he knew that he lived here only by a kind of sufferance, that if he incurred the enmity of the Box S his days in Toprock were indeed numbered.

He said again, 'I was just trying to help. You tell your father that. This girl knows where Belmont and the kid are hiding. I'll bet on it.'

'I'll talk to her.' Helen Sellers dismissed him as finally as if she had ordered him away.

He shifted from one foot to the other, uncertainly, then realizing that she was not going to move until he was gone, he turned and disappeared through the rear door of the store.

15.

The girl still crouched on the ground, nursing her twisted arm, her dark eyes turned upward as she watched Helen with the wariness of a hurt animal.

Helen said, 'How badly are you hurt?' Her tone was cool, a little impersonal. She had been raised in a land where minor bodily injuries were a part of the day's work.

The girl shook her head. She got slowly to her feet, still nursing the twisted arm.

149

'What's your name?'

'Mary Lu Walker.'

'Do you know who I am?'

The girl nodded, and the gesture held a slight trace of defiance.

'Can you pick up that sack and hand it to me?'

Mary Lu answered by hoisting the half filled sack until Helen could reach it. She slung it across her saddle. 'Now, where do you live?'

Mary Lu turned and pointed to the Walker cabin, barely visible among the trees.

'All right, let's go over there. Lead the way.'

The Walker girl hesitated, and it was obvious that she wanted to refuse but did not quite dare. She turned and moved off, and Helen kneed her horse forward to follow. When the girl reached the corner of the cabin she stopped, looking around at Helen Sellers.

Helen Sellers glanced about her, at the trees and brush, and finally at the cabin. 'Anyone in there?'

Mary Lu shook her head. 'Pa's in Stanton getting drunk.' She said it without feeling or apology, as if she accepted it as a part of life.

Helen Sellers noted the much-washed dress, the broken boots she wore, and a feeling of sympathy rose through her, a feeling which she put away because she knew that she had to force this girl to talk, and she realized that it would not be easy.

150

She said, 'These groceries,' and indicated the sack which was still propped across her saddle bow, 'they are for Belmont and the boy with him?'

The girl merely looked at her, her expression vacant.

Helen nodded, and her tone changed, becoming almost confidential. 'There's no reason why you should trust me. If the positions were reversed I certainly would not trust you, but do you know that it was I who got Belmont and Davey out of jail in Stanton and sent them to Wolfson's ranch?'

At mention of Claude Wolfson, the girl's dark eyes flashed with anger for a moment, then dulled. Helen, watching her closely, noted this and did not understand, but she went on.

'I know quite a lot about this, and I'm sorry for the whole business.'

'They didn't have to hang Davey's father.' It was the first real feeling Mary Lu had permitted herself.

'I know. It was an accident and . . .'

'And he's dead.' Now that the dam was broken, words piled out of her. 'And Davey would be dead. Honest John and Bronc Charley would have killed him, and no one— not anyone—tried to help . . . no one but Belmont. I saw it.' She poured out the whole story of how Bronc Charley had been killed.

The sense of shame which had been

smoldering within Helen Sellers for three days broke into flame. 'I know they need friends. That's the reason I'm trying to help.'

'Help?' The girl's young voice dripped with scorn. 'Help? You want me to tell you where they are so you can lead your father to them, so that he can get back his gold.'

Helen controlled herself with an effort. She knew that somehow she had to win over this girl if she had any real hope of helping the boy and Belmont, and for some reason which she could not quite explain to herself, that had become for her the most important thing in life.

She dismounted, dropping the sack of groceries to the ground. 'I met Belmont when he was riding away from the Wolfson ranch,' she said steadily. 'He could have been riding out of this country to safety for himself. There was no reason why he should come back to Toprock. He owed nothing to Davey Berry or to any of us. I told him so.'

Mary Lu stared at her with questioning eyes.

'And I learned something,' Helen told her, 'something about the country, and about myself. I learned something from this drifter whom I knew nothing about, who was a stranger, a wanderer—perhaps a murderer.'

'You love him?' the mountain girl asked suddenly.

'Love him?' The question took Helen

152

Sellers entirely by surprise. She had not, she realized now, actually looked on Belmont as a person at all. To her he had merely represented an idea, the idea of someone unselfishly helping those who needed help. 'I don't even know him,' she said, dismissing the whole thing with a tiny wave of one hand.

'I love him,' said Mary Lu very seriously. Suddenly, the wall which she had held between herself and the other woman had fallen away. 'I love him very much. He is strong and kind and brave, and he has suffered.'

'Suffered?'

'Davey told me. He shot a man because of a girl—down in Texas—and the girl would have nothing to do with him. You can see it in his eyes. They look sad.'

Helen Sellers considered. Belmont's eyes had held a shadow of sadness.

'And he was good to Davey. Davey would have been in plenty of trouble if Belmont hadn't shot Bronc Charley.'

Helen Sellers wondered what this mountain girl considered trouble. It seemed to her that with the whole country engaged in one of the largest manhunts of basin history, both Davey and Belmont were in about as deep trouble as she could imagine.

'Davey was just ready to go bad.' The girl spoke about the fifteen-year-old as if he were full-grown, a man. 'He might even go bad yet, but Belmont won't let him.'

153

'All right.' Helen Sellers' tone was businesslike. She found that it embarrassed her to hear this girl talk about her feelings for Belmont. She wondered how old she was. She supposed that probably this would be a proper match—the mountain girl and the drifter. But certainly the girl was too young, and yet, they married young in the hills. Belmont and this waif . . . For some reason she did not like the thought.

'You know where they are?'

Mary Lu's eyes turned blank. 'I didn't say that.' Her tone was a denial.

Helen tried to hold her patience. 'Sure you know. You must, or you wouldn't have been stealing the food for them.'

Mary Lu glanced at the sack of food, and then away.

'Look,' said Helen, and reached out both hands to grasp the girl's slight shoulders. 'For their sake you have to believe me. They need help. Every man my father could hire or could persuade is out with one of the posse. They're combing the whole basin, and they'll keep on hunting until they find them. We've only one chance. If I can locate them—if I can get them to Claude Wolfson's ranch—they'll be safe.'

At mention of Wolfson, the younger girl, who had been standing quiet in her grasp, twisted away. 'Wolfson? What kind of a fool do you take me for? It was Wolfson's men who ambushed us when we came up out of Black

Canyon. It was Wolfson's men who shot my horse. If it hadn't been for them we'd all have been miles away from here by now.'

Helen gasped. 'You must be mistaken.'

'Mistaken, am I? I don't make that kind of mistake. I've watched the Wolfson crew riding through the brush until I could recognize each and every one of them. I've seen them slip into Toprock and make their small deals with Honest John, and that isn't all. I heard them shouting to Belmont to surrender, telling him exactly who they were.'

The force of the younger girl's anger made Helen Sellers realize that Mary Lu must be telling the truth. There was nothing to make the girl lie about this, but her mind refused to accept the implication.

'You say they were waiting, that it was an ambush, that it did not happen by accident?'

Passionately Mary Lu told her exactly what had happened. She ended by saying, 'They were waiting for us. They shot my horse without any warning and scattered what food we had all over the ground.'

Helen thought bitterly, Claude's crew must be double-crossing him. They must be after the gold for themselves. But how did they hear that Belmont was being hunted? She was very sure that the news had not come to them from the sheriff or from her father. Perhaps one of Wolfson's men had been in Stanton when Honest John rode in, and had heard the talk and carried it back to the ranch.

But this she doubted. She felt that if this had happened Wolfson would have known all about it before she rode out to tell him, and Wolfson certainly would not have pretended ignorance had he already known. Why should he? She puzzled over the problem, deciding that Wolfson must have told the crew and that some of them, on their own, had taken off with the idea of capturing Belmont and getting the gold.

Knowing the rag-tail crew for what they were, this did not surprise her, but her anger rose. In a way this ambush was her fault. If she had not carried the word of the manhunt to the ranch they would not have known in time to plant the ambush. She had tried to help, and she had only succeeded in making things worse for the fugitives. This knowledge now strengthened her resolve to assist.

She said briskly, 'All right. We can't take them to the Wolfson ranch, but we can get them out of the country.'

The girl stared at her. 'How?'

She said with more confidence than she really felt, 'I'm coming with you. No one in this country is going to do anything to you or to them as long as I am there.' She had her reservations on this. Probably most of the man-hunters would hesitate before they attacked a party which included the daughter of the Box S. It would only be if she ran into her own father that she would find real trouble.

'Where are they?'

Mary Lu hesitated. It wasn't that she did not trust this other girl. But never before in her life had she been called upon to make so great a decision—a decision which might mean the capture and hanging of a man. And suddenly she was feeling very young and helpless and alone.

'I'm to meet them at the Devil's Needle,' she said. 'There's a cave in the side canyon about a quarter of a mile from the Needle. Davey knows where it is. We found it one day last year, but we'll have to go around through the upper basin. The sheriff and his men crossed the canyon this morning. They're on the west side somewhere.'

Helen Sellers considered. 'My father was not with them?'

The girl shook her head. 'The Toprock people would have told me if your father had been here. Ab Sellers was not mentioned.'

'All right,' said Helen. 'Have you got a horse?'

'I can borrow one.'

'Borrow it then and we will start back along the Stanton road. It will be better for us if your Honest John thinks we returned to Stanton.' She glanced at the grocery sack. 'And we can pack that stuff in the saddlebags so people will not see what we are carrying—

or rather, we'll leave it here.'

'Here?' Mary Lu's eyes widened. 'You mean we're not to take the food to them?'

'I've a better idea,' Helen said. 'No, take it along. We may need it after all.'

Mary Lu was uncertain, not sure what she meant, and very uneasy because of her uncertainty. But she did not know how to refuse. She went after her horse and returned to find Helen already packing the food into her saddlebags.

Together they rode down the trail toward Stanton, and just before they dropped over the rise Mary Lu looked back at Toprock. The town still held its bleak, deserted look, but one man watched them with an intentness which sent a nervous chill along her spine. Honest John stood in the store doorway, his face expressionless, his eyes never leaving them.

Halfway to Stanton they came off the grade onto the floor of the basin proper, and Helen Sellers, in the lead, swung her horse westward across the rolling ground toward the banks of the Black River.

At the point where they reached the stream, a good half mile south of the canyon mouth, the river no longer raged among the boulders but ran through earth cutbanks, a channel some eight feet wide, its water a kind of dull brown, colored by the pine needles through which it had soaked.

They crossed, glancing upward toward the

158

mouth of the canyon above them, then followed the swelling rise of the hill line west toward where the sun was setting behind the snow-covered peaks.

With the coming of darkness, the air chilled down to a near freezing point and grew penetrating as they climbed again into the rough country bordering the basin to the west.

The moon was late in rising and it was dark in the timber, but both girls knew the country from long experience and they pushed on steadily, trusting their horses not to stumble into some unseen crevasse. The moon came up finally, a sliver out of the dark sky which gave only a little light.

The Devil's Needle by straight crow's flight was less than fifteen miles west of the river, but they had covered nearly twenty miles and were still a good five miles short of their objective, when they worked their way out of the timber and saw above them the white gleam of the snow fields in the faint moonlight, and then, far off to the right, the low yellow glow of a fire.

At once Mary Lu, who had been riding in front, halted her horse, gazing at the distant fire with narrow eyes as she waited for Helen Sellers to pull abreast. When the older girl came up she pointed toward the light.

'Sheriff's men.'

Helen Sellers sounded unexcited. 'I thought they'd be along here somewhere. Let's ride over and have a look.'

The younger girl tensed in her saddle, twisting to face her companion. 'What are you up to? What are you trying to do?'

For an instant Helen hesitated. Then she said steadily, 'I didn't tell you before because I was certain what you would say. You didn't know me well enough to trust me.'

'I don't now.' The younger girl's voice was full of bitterness.

'You have to,' Helen Sellers told her, 'because you haven't much choice. At first I meant to ride out here with you to get the supplies to Belmont and the boy, so that they might have their chance to work through those mountains.' She indicated the snowy peaks. 'But have you ever tried to ride through up there? I have, but not at this time of year. Even in late summer it's nearly impossible. Now they wouldn't stand one chance in a thousand of coming through alive.'

The younger girl still sounded bitter. 'Anything is better than hanging.'

'No one is going to hang. I knew that as soon as you told me about the killing of Bronc Charley. Honest John told his version of the story, figuring that the only other witness was the boy, not knowing that you were hiding in the timber seeing everything that happened. Now it will be three people's testimony to one—yours, Davey's and Belmont's.'

'Won't make a bit of difference.'

Helen Sellers looked at the other girl with a certain feeling of helplessness. She knew how Mary Lu felt, and she could not blame her. All this girl's life she had feared the law and seen her friends harried by it, driven by it.

'It will.' She said this confidently. 'Don't forget, I'm on your side. I'll see that Belmont gets a fair trial. I'll see that no one bothers Davey.'

Mary Lu was still unconvinced. 'What about your Daddy?'

Helen Sellers thought grimly that this was the crux of the problem. What about her father? She said with determination, 'Let me handle him. I can handle the sheriff and the judge—yes, and my father.' She did not continue the argument, but swung her horse, riding toward the distant fire.

The other girl hesitated for a moment, then went in pursuit. She did not know what else to do.

16.

Claude Wolfson was not a man to let his anger show easily. For nearly his full life he had practiced self-control, but as he listened to Ben August and DeVoto report the failure of their attack on Belmont, it was all he could do to keep from striking them.

161

'So, he got through, and you don't know where he is now?' He dismissed them with a gesture of his hand, and stood staring out at the rising swell of the mountains. Belmont could be anywhere, and the only chance that remained to catch him was if the tracker could stay on his trail.

Coming to a sudden resolve, Wolfson stepped out into the yard and saw August and DeVoto beside the cook shack and went to them.

'The rest of the crew is in the hills back of the ranch. I'm going to town. You ride in with me, August.' He turned to the corral then, catching up his horse and saddling it. It was a matter of pride with him that he could do anything about the ranch as well as or better than the men he employed.

All during the ride to Stanton he held his silence, and Ben August, feeling the weight of his displeasure, did not try to ride abreast but held his own horse a good length behind that of his employer. They crossed the badlands and followed the road in its long stretch over the level of the valley toward the tree-fringed course of the river, crossing the stream by the bridge from which Dave Berry had swung to his death, and thus they came into the dust ribbon which was Stanton's main street.

In the town's largest saloon he leaned against the bar with Ben August at his side and listened to the gossip which flowed throughout the smoky room. He took no part in the conversation, leaning with both elbows on the bar, his shoulders hunched, his hat drawn down a little so that it shielded his handsome face.

Despite his time in the basin, he knew that in certain senses he was an outsider and that Stanton was not his town. He heard the wild rumors which flowed in and out of the batwing doors. There was one story that Belmont had been cornered by the sheriff's men, another that he had been seen far to the southeast, but through it all Wolfson noticed that there was an air of dissatisfaction in the room.

These people, mostly townsmen—since the majority of the basin's riders had joined the manhunt—did not like Ab Sellers. They bowed to his dictates since they were afraid of his power, but more than one of them made slurring remarks which showed that their actual sympathies were with the unknown drifter who was being hunted so relentlessly.

Claude Wolfson listened, and weighed the temper of the crowd, savoring it, wondering how he could turn it to his advantage, for he still meant to wrest control of this country from Sellers when the proper moment arrived.

Finally he cautioned Ben August against too much drink and turned out of the saloon. Evening had arrived and the street was near darkness, relieved only by the lamplight which glowed from the store windows.

163

It was the supper hour, and there were few people upon the street as Wolfson made his way to the hotel and into the lobby. He glanced through the dining room door as he passed, failed to see Helen Sellers in the big room and hesitated. Then he moved on to the high desk where he asked Portal Holmes, the clerk, for his usual room, and after he had been handed his key said in a careless voice, 'Is Miss Sellers in her room?'

The clerk glanced at the board on the wall behind the desk where the room keys hung in ordered rows, and shook his head.

'Her key is here.'

A voice behind Wolfson said, 'I want to talk to you,' and Wolfson turned and found himself staring upward into Ab Sellers' hard eyes.

The rancher stood on the stairs which mounted alongside the far wall to the upper floor, his small body looking thin and whip-like under his neat black coat.

He came down slowly. There was something arrogant in the way he walked and in the way he held his small head. Years of command had left their mark in haughty intolerance, and this intolerance showed in his tone as he faced Wolfson. He glanced at the clerk, and Portal Holmes read the order in the imperious eyes and slipped away through the door which led to the small office behind the lobby.

They were alone, although the sound of

164

voices and the rattle of silver on crockery reached them through the open dining room door.

'I should have run you out of the valley when you first showed up.' It was a statement, not a threat.

Wolfson knew that the older man was studying him, and the thought brought a touch of amusement which he was quick to conceal. He did not argue. He was interested in what Sellers might have to say. It was one of the few times in their acquaintanceship that Sellers had ever purposely sought him out, and the action brought certain possibilities to his mind.

'You were asking for my daughter. I have warned you before to stay away from her.'

Still Wolfson did not speak. His years of gambling had taught him never to expose a hand until he had seen the other man's cards. He waited.

'She isn't here,' the rancher said. 'I've asked the liveryman. He tells me that she rode out on the Toprock road.'

Wolfson was startled, but tried not to show it.

'I thought you might know where she is.' There was a trace of malice in the older man's eyes.

Wolfson had a very good idea, and suddenly he was raging inside, but he still did not show it by any change of expression.

165

Sellers' tone was suddenly bitter. 'This is your fault,' he said. 'If you hadn't helped her get that drifter out of jail, none of this would have happened. I've watched you for some time, Wolfson. I know you and your kind. You're greedy and grasping, and you'll stop at nothing to get what you want. But I tell you this.

'First, you'll never marry my daughter, and second, as soon as this other business is cleared up you are going to leave the basin. Put a price on your place. I'll buy it—anything within reason. Or, if you'd rather fight, I'll step on you as if you were an ant. Good night.' He walked across the lobby then and disappeared into the dining room.

Wolfson watched him go. Rage came up to cloud the sharpness of his mind and leave a bitter taste of gall deep in his mouth. He hated Sellers, but suddenly his hatred of the banker was as nothing compared to his feeling about Belmont.

He had had things under easy control. Years of careful planning had put him close to the position which he wanted, and then all in a few days this whole structure seemed to be crumbling beneath him, and all because a chance rider, headed nowhere, had happened to ride into the basin.

He went on up to his room. He had no desire for dinner. He had no desire to stand around the saloon and listen to the speculations of the townsmen about the manhunt. He wanted to think, but also he wanted to be alone, to try to adjust his sights to meet this new threat to his hopes and plans.

Most of all, he wanted to talk to Helen Sellers. He was enough of an egoist to still believe that, given an hour alone with the girl, he could convince her that her interest in this tramp rider was both silly and dangerous.

The window of his room overlooked the main street. He drew a chair before it and sat waiting for her return. Every time a horse came down the Toprock road he straightened, peering into the night, but as the sky lightened and the sun came up to announce the arrival of morning, he had seen no sign of her. But still he did not stir. He held his place until the sheriff's posse rode into town, glancing at his watch then, surprised that it was nearly ten.

Sellers came down from the hotel porch, and Wolfson could hear plainly as the rancher talked with the man in charge. His lips tightened as he heard the man say, 'Your daughter and another girl came to our camp, late last night. They talked to Glass and made a deal, promising that if Glass sent us home they would surrender Belmont and the boy.'

Wolfson could not hear Sellers' low-voiced reply, nor did he wait. He rose and went downstairs, seeking Ben August in the hotel bar, and sent him riding to the ranch with orders to bring in the full crew.

167

17.

Belmont roused with the first light and lay for a moment shivering under the protection of the single blanket. They had not dared build a fire and the shallow cave was little warmer than an icebox, but the roof was high and it was large enough so that they had brought the horses in for concealment.

They had reached the Needle during the preceding afternoon. It was merely an upthrust of bare rock which rose from the slope of the mountain like a finger pointing at the sky.

Not spectacular, only some thirty feet higher than the surrounding slope, it still was a clear landmark, and he could understand why Davey and the girl had chosen it as a meeting place. It was easy to find, even in the rough country which surrounded it, and that was important since each side canyon resembled another, and to lose your way was one of the dangers of trying to travel this land.

They had reached the cave, firmly confident that they had so well hidden their tracks that their pursuers would have difficulty in finding them in this waste, and then at nightfall they had worked back down the canyon and climbed the Needle for a look at the country below them, and had spotted the light of the sheriff's fire.

Even, Belmont had been surprised that the sheriff's men were so closely on their heels, and turning to study the snowy slopes above them had been filled with his first real sense of futility. Someone was leading the posse—someone who seemed to be able to read their sign.

He had kept watch through the first part of the night while the boy slept. He would have let Davey sleep until daylight, but he knew the value of pride. Far better that the boy should lose a few hours sleep than that he should feel he was a burden to the man, that he was not pulling his own weight.

He moved out then, and found the small figure in its niche halfway up the canyon side, flanked by a row of rocks, and called softly.

Davey stirred and stood up. His small body had been wrapped in his blanket, but despite the covering his thin face was blue with cold and his teeth rattled a little as he slid down to join Belmont.

'See anything?'

The boy shook his head. Belmont was staring down at him, thoughtfully, wondering if they dared chance a fire. Once the sun climbed enough to dump its heat into this narrow canyon things would not be too bad, but it would be a full two hours before it rose high enough to clear the rim.

He debated, considering what to do. Mary

169

Lu, according to the boy, should have been here before daylight. Since she wasn't, it might mean that she was not coming. He did not doubt that she had tried, and that something had stopped her. Perhaps she had run into the sheriff's men . . . Perhaps . . . But what was the use of speculating? The problem was to decide what to do now.

They could get out the horses and start up the side canyon. The boy said that it would lead them toward the top, but he had no idea how deep the snow would be up there, no idea how many miles it was across the snow fields, nor would he know until they could see the lower reaches of the slopes on the far side. With food they might possibly make it. Without, there was small chance. Already, it was nearly twenty-four hours since either of them had eaten.

And then he was suddenly alert, for faintly, carried by the upthrust of the morning wind, he heard a thin halloo. He could not tell whether it had been made by a man or woman. The sound was far distant and vague, like an echo which has rebounded once too often from its reflecting rocks.

He swung around, peering down the canyon, and then said across his shoulder to the shivering boy, 'Go on up to the cave. Saddle the horses and be ready to move out. Stand between them. You'll get a little heat from their bodies.'

He did not wait for the boy's answer, but moved quickly through the canyon to the turn above the Needle. Here he scrambled up the rough rock wall, finding craggy handholds to help his ascent.

He perched here on a shelf so narrow that he had to lean backward against the mountain's slope to keep from falling, and stared out at the land around the Needle. It was nearly bare rock, supporting so little vegetation that there was no cover for a horse. Below the Needle, moving toward him, he made out two riders.

At the distance, and with the rising sun at their backs, it was impossible to tell who they were, but the very fact that there were two rather than a single girl was a warning in itself. His first unreasoning impulse was to turn and run. This was sheer instinct, the heritage of countless generations when early man was a fugitive beset by dangers on every side. But reason held him where he was.

There were only two. He could see across the rocky slope for nearly five uninterrupted miles. There were crevices, of course, and shallow washes where melted snow water had tracked out its path down through the boulders. But he had traveled that same ground on the preceding afternoon, and he was more than certain that no rider could approach the Needle without being seen from above.

171

He waited then, gripping the chill metal of his rifle, in his tenseness failing to notice the cold, and he saw the riders grow slowly in size as they mounted toward him, but even when they reached the base of the Needle and came around it he was not certain who they were.

Still he felt confident that if there were only two he could handle the situation. He saw them round the rock's base, now out of the glare of the sun, and he was certain that the one in the lead was Mary Lu, but could not guess the identity of her companion.

He thought—and put the thought away as an absurd thing—that the second rider was also a girl, but he did not actually know until they reached the mouth of the canyon itself, now scarcely half a mile below him. They halted here, and again the cry rose through the morning air, this time clear and unmistakable—a woman's voice, calling his name.

Unconsciously his eyes went out beyond them to search the land up which they had come, to hunt for movement showing that this was some kind of a trap. But there was none, and he made his decision, dropping down from his perch in a quickening slide, almost a fall, to stand in the canyon's stony bottom, where the narrow cut made its looping, concealing turn. He moved around this turn and saw them riding up toward him, and with a sense of unexpected shock recognized the

172

second rider as Helen Sellers.

He stood motionless, the rifle in the crook of his arm, watching their approach, his face immobile in the morning light, as if it had been carved from the rock which towered above them.

He expected Mary Lu to explain, but it was Helen Sellers who swung down first, Helen Sellers who walked to him, looking at him with the curiosity of a total stranger.

She wasted few words. She said, 'Mary Lu would have been here sooner if I had let her come. I made her stop at the sheriff's fire.'

She studied his face as she said this, expecting his expression to break, but he showed no surprise, no feeling, and she thought—he has himself under complete control. Nothing I could say would shake him, nothing would break his reserve. She thought that few men acquired such reserve without embittering experience. She found the thought unpleasant and put it away from her, telling herself that she neither knew nor cared what his past life had been.

She said, 'Mary Lu was very doubtful about it, but she rode with me because she had no choice. She did not believe you stood the chance of justice from the sheriff. I told her that you did, that Barney Glass would listen to me.'

Still Belmont stood quiet, his rifle cradled, his eyes steady and unreadable upon her face.

173

She felt a certain rising annoyance. He might at least show a trace of curiosity.

'I told the sheriff,' she said, 'that I had two witnesses who would make a liar out of Honest John. I told him that you did not murder Bronc Charley, that you shot him in self-defense. I also told him that if he would send his posse back to town and wait at the camp by himself, I'd ride up here and bring you in.'

For the first time Belmont's face showed a trace of emotion, amusement. It glittered in his eyes. 'You must be a convincing talker, ma'am.'

She flushed a little then, but she met his look levelly. 'I can always convince Barney Glass of anything. He's in love with me.'

'Well,' said Belmont, 'that is something any man should understand.'

Her flush deepened, but her voice was even when she said, 'Of course, you aren't in any way bound by what I told him. There is some food in these saddlebags. You are free to take it and ride on up this canyon. If you can get through the snow you'll be safe enough. No one will follow you across that, but I banked on the fact that you'd rather clear yourself of this absurd charge, that given a chance you'd stay and fight rather than run away.'

'Don't listen!' Mary Lu pushed forward. 'Oh, she means all right, but she just doesn't understand. She's never been forced to fight

174

her father. She doesn't know what a horrible man he is.'

Belmont looked from one to the other, and the corners of his mouth quirked a little. 'Let's go up to the cave and let Davey decide. This is his problem too.'

Helen Sellers started to protest, then thought better of it and held her peace. Belmont turned, leading the way, calling Davey's name as they came in sight of the cave. The boy's head appeared, and he said, 'Get a fire going, Davey. We'll have some coffee in a jiffy.'

The boy looked at him, startled by mention of the fire, looked at the two girls, hesitated, then turned and disappeared. Before they had climbed to the cave entrance, he had gathered a few dry straws from the rock crevices and had a small blaze going.

There was very little wood, twisted branches from the dwarfed cedars which somehow found a footing in the earth-filled cracks, but there was enough to warm the cave somewhat, to heat the coffee brewed in the battered pan with snow water, melted from the patch above them.

The hot liquid brought faint color to the boy's white, pinched cheeks, to his bluish lips. He drank silently, supping at the liquid so hot that it nearly scalded him, and ate wolfishly of the cold meat and dry biscuits.

No one spoke. Belmont had not mentioned

Helen Sellers' proposition since reaching the cave. He had not explained her surprising presence, and Davey had not asked.

The man ate also, slower than the boy, seeming to treat each bite with care and relish, a relish that only those who have known deep hunger can appreciate. Neither girl touched the food, although Helen did drink a small amount of the black, unsweetened coffee.

Not until Davey had finished and licked the last grease from his fingers did Belmont say, 'I suppose you're wondering what Miss Sellers is doing here. She is here to rescue us again as she did that night from the jail.'

The boy stared at him and then slowly turned his dark eyes on the girl. He said in a considered tone, 'Why should she?' There was suspicion buried deep in his voice.

'A good question,' Belmont agreed, and smiled openly, the first time Helen had seen him smile so. It lighted his whole face, softening it, giving it a touch of friendly warmth. 'But we have no right to question her motives, which I am sure are perfectly solid in her own eyes. Already we're indebted to her for this breakfast. She has pulled the pursuers off our trail so that we dare to build a fire.'

The boy was not understanding. His head twisted one way and then the other. Belmont seemed to take pity on his uncertainty.

He said in a tone which no longer held a trace of mockery, 'It's this way, Dave. You and

176

Mary Lu were present when Bronc Charley died. You can testify before the judge that my shot was fired in self-defense.'

At mention of the judge, the boy seemed to freeze. His eyes fell and he stared fixedly at the stone beneath his feet. For a long moment there was silence in the cave, save for the stamp of the restless horses.

'Dave,' said Belmont, 'there comes a time in every man's life when he has to face up to things if he ever means to stop running. I don't blame you for not trusting the people in Stanton after what has happened, but you've no reason to mistrust Miss Sellers. She's fronted for us twice now, and I figure that she'll front for us again. She wants us to ride over to the sheriff's fire and give ourselves up to him. They'll take us to town, and there will be a preliminary hearing before the judge. She thinks it won't even come to trial.'

The boy looked up, straight into Belmont's eyes. His chin wobbled a little, but his words were steady enough. 'Is that what you want?'

Belmont said, 'It isn't what I want that matters in this case, Davey. It's what you want. We can try to get up through the snow if you want to. We aren't bound by Miss Sellers' word.'

'Her word?' Davey stared at him.

'She gave her word to the sheriff that she would bring us in. He believed her enough so that he sent his posse back to town. If we go on, he'll be in trouble and she'll be in trouble, but after all, that isn't our business, is it? Our business is to take care of ourselves.'

The boy stirred. He stood up. He walked toward the entrance of the cave. Mary Lu spoke to him but he shook his head. He stepped outside and stayed for several minutes. Inside no one spoke. Finally he came back. 'This ain't your trouble.' He was speaking to Belmont. 'You got into this on account of me. I guess it's up to me to see you out of it. I guess there ain't much I can do but ride in and tell my story to the judge.'

Coming down from the Needle, Mary Lu and the boy rode in front, Helen Sellers and Belmont following. The morning was still chill, the air so clear that the ridged mountains behind them seemed etched against the blue crystal of the sky.

Belmont was quiet, Helen Sellers a little restless in her saddle, watching the two ahead, watching the slope below them, saying finally, 'The change in the boy is remarkable.'

Belmont turned to look at her. He had been studying her without appearing to, all the way down the canyon.

She flushed under his eyes. 'I mean that when I got you out of jail the other night he trusted no one. Now he is willing to ride in because he thinks it is best for you. Last week he would not have cared.'

Belmont said nothing.

'And you've affected other people in the

178

basin, people who have hardly seen you, people in Stanton. I listened to them yesterday. The livery man, the saddle maker. They are pulling for you to get away, to beat my father. I don't think the country will be the same after your passing.'

'Passing?'

'I mean after you ride on.' Her color had deepened, and she was no longer looking at him. 'You are going to ride on, aren't you?'

'I suppose so, if they let me.'

'Over the next hill,' she said, 'through the next town. What is it you're hunting?'

He did not know. He had not known for a long time. 'Maybe I'm just a drifter, a weed that rolls away before the wind, the south wind.' He added this last with a wry smile.

'Do you think I did right in bringing you in—in keeping you from trying to cross the mountains?'

He shrugged.

'If I am wrong, if I've gotten you into worse trouble, I'll not forgive myself.'

He did not answer directly. He said, 'There's the sheriff's camp.' His tone suggested that it was too late for doubts, that the cards were drawn, the play already made.

He saw Barney Glass' big shape against the morning sun and knew that the man was nervous for all his outward sureness, and smiled a little to himself as they pulled up their horses.

179

Glass' relief showed in every line of his body. For three hours he had waited here, cursing Helen Sellers and her persuasive tone. He had died a hundred times, knowing what Ab Sellers would say if the girl was wrong, if Belmont and the boy refused to come in but chose rather to ride away.

He was almost friendly with relief as he walked over to Belmont, saying as he came, 'I'll have to take your guns.'

Belmont sat loose in the saddle, looking smaller than he really was on the high back of his big horse.

'No,' he said.

The word ran like a shock through the sheriff's body, grinding all the good humor out of him. He stopped, and his handsome face tightened, and he said doggedly, 'I've got to take your guns. What would it look like, bringing in a prisoner armed?'

Belmont's mouth corners tugged upward. He knew that to Barney Glass appearances were more important than actions, but he refused to bow to the man's vanity. 'I'm coming in voluntarily,' he stressed the last word, 'not as a prisoner. I'm riding in to clear up a misunderstanding, and I'll keep my guns—that is, unless you want to take them away from me.'

He saw the raw desire grow in the sheriff's eyes, and knew that the boy had shifted so that he was behind the sheriff and to one side.

180

Barney Glass knew this also, and knew that he was whipsawed, and cursed himself for ever getting into this spot.

Helen Sellers saw what had happened, and realized what it might lead to. Barney Glass was a man who lived by his pride. Take that from him, and there was little save an empty shell.

She pushed her horse forward, giving him an out, giving him the chance he needed to back down gracefully. 'Barney, stop it! You promised I could bring them in. Remember?'

He looked at her then, and his thinking processes were a little too sluggish to know that she did this purposely. He said with a kind of sullen relief, 'I'm sorry. I forgot. Tell this man not to cross me if he doesn't want to get hurt.' He swung away then, moving stiff-legged over to his horse.

For an instant Helen Sellers' eyes found those of Belmont, and in that instant a message flashed between them, and there was a solider understanding than there had been before.

They rode, Glass ahead, still nursing his battered feelings, Davey and Mary Lu, and finally Belmont and the girl. There was no pretense that they were prisoners. They were coming in because they wished. This, Belmont understood, was how it had to be. Not that he was trying to act like Glass, riding his feelings. It was the effect upon the town that they had to achieve, the feeling that they had not been dragged as criminals before the bar of justice, but had chosen to come in, ready to prove their innocence.

Helen murmured, 'That was close. Don't push him when it isn't necessary. He is a small boy, wearing a chip on his shoulder, called upon to prove his strength.'

Belmont did not answer.

'When you ride on,' she said, 'will you take the boy with you?'

'If he wants to go. The choice is his.'

'And the girl?'

Belmont looked around, startled. 'The girl . . . you know I can't do that. The trail is no place for her.'

'She's in love with you.'

He turned his head and started to laugh.

'She told me.'

The laughter went away. 'A crazy kid.' He said it half under his breath. 'She's like the boy, romantic notions in her head. He tried to compare me to Billy the Kid.'

Her voice was serious. 'She's young, but age doesn't make a woman. Some mature younger than others. They have to.'

Belmont had the sensation that he was within a room, a small room, and that the walls were gradually folding in upon him, enclosing him. He said in a kind of strangled protest, 'I can't be responsible for every maverick along the trail. Forget it. She'll get

182

over it.'

He pushed ahead then. He did not want to hear anything more that Helen Sellers said. There was something about her which disturbed him, disturbed him more than did the sheriff's guns.

They came into Stanton in the early afternoon, just as the day's single train was puffing its way out from the station platform, and the fact that most of the town's citizens used the train's arrival as a signal to journey toward the station rather spoiled the effect of their entrance.

But Ab Sellers was on the hotel porch waiting to receive them, and he came down the steps and stood on the board sidewalk, his small body ramrod straight, his face looking mask-like as if it were carved stone.

He ignored his daughter. He ignored the boy and Mary Lu, concentrating his attention on the sheriff and Belmont who rode side by side.

He said to the sheriff in his tight voice, 'What's the prisoner doing with his guns?'

Belmont sat for a moment where he was. Sellers' question had been directed to Glass, but the old eyes, frosty with dislike, were fixed on him. He swung down, walking deliberately around the horse to fasten the reins, then he came up onto the sidewalk so that he towered above Sellers.

'I'm not a prisoner.' He said, this mildly, as

183

if he were merely remarking upon the weather. 'I rode in because I wanted to, and I wear my guns because I want to. I let you take them once. I won't make that mistake again.'

No one had spoken thus to Ab Sellers in over thirty years. His face flushed and then went dead white under his heavy tan. 'We'll see about that. You're in my town, young man. Do you know what that means, my town?'

'Old man,' said Belmont, 'it might have been your town once, when you were strong enough to hold it, but it isn't now. You've cast a long shadow here.' Inwardly he was furious. The idea that Sellers or anyone like him could so browbeat a community that he could claim it as his very own, built up in Belmont a stubborn resistance which knew little reason. But none of this showed in his voice.

The sheriff, who had also dismounted, shifted uneasily, and Belmont's voice struck out at him like a snake. 'Careful. Don't get into this.'

They were frozen, Ab Sellers by utter disbelief, Glass by horror that anyone in the world would dare to talk to Sellers thus.

Belmont said, 'You parade your law. You send out and arrest me on no better grounds than that someone thinks I might have had something to do with Dave Berry in that stage holdup. You listen to Honest John, and turn the whole countryside loose to hunt me for the killing of Bronc Charley. And yet, you and

184

your town hanged an innocent man, and not one of you was so much as rebuked.'

Sellers seemed to be strangling as he tried to get his words out. Belmont said, 'I've had a bellyful of all of you. Where's this judge, sheriff, that you want me to appear before, or do I have to hunt him up myself?'

The sheriff licked his lips. He glanced at Ab Sellers and found the old rancher staring at him with open contempt.

Sellers had mastered his breath. 'All right,' he said. 'Go on. Go on.'

The sheriff turned upward toward the courthouse, wishing at the moment that he was a thousand miles away. The boy swung down, carrying his rifle. After a single glance Belmont ignored it, making no protest. Together they went up the walk. Helen Sellers dismounted, motioning Mary Lu out of her saddle.

Her father, who had not moved, stared at Helen hard. 'Where do you think you're going?'

She met his eyes squarely. Once, when she was smaller, she would have cowered before him, accepting in silence his tirades, but that time was gone.

'To the courthouse.'

He spat in the dust at his feet. 'No decent woman monkeys in men's affairs.'

She said without heat, 'Perhaps if you'd asked me you would not be in this trouble.'

'I'm in no trouble.'

'I think you are,' she said. 'You've dominated this town a long time—so long that you've ceased to listen to what people are saying. But I've been listening these last few days. A week ago Dave Berry could not have found one friend in the whole of Stanton. Alive, he meant nothing. Dead, he has become a kind of symbol, and that man who just left us is becoming the same thing. Yesterday he was unknown, but you made him known by sending your watchdogs out to hunt him down. Today a good half of the people in the basin are praying that he will escape.'

Her father glared at her and spat again. 'A murderer. The court will take care of him.'

She shook her head. 'I have a witness here to prove that you are wrong. Come, Mary Lu.' She took the younger girl's arm and moved down the street toward the courthouse. The people coming back from watching the train depart looked at them and looked at the sheriff moving beside Belmont, and a murmur rose through the crowd, and soon a good half of the citizens of the town were headed for the court. But Claude Wolfson, who had witnessed it all through the hotel window, did not join them. Instead he moved out onto the hotel porch, finding a seat at the sheltered end, content to wait.

186

18.

Judge Lister Crane was nearly seventy years old. A spare man, he had been a circuit rider for thirty years, carrying the torch of justice to a rough segment of the territory a hundred miles across.

He was a terse man and a hard one, and one who had never flinched from what he considered his duty. He had clashed before with Ab Sellers, and there was small love between them. The sheriff he regarded as a bumptious child, an overgrown boy whose strutting annoyed him, whose posturing made him ill.

He sat now at his desk at the end of the dusty courtroom, staring out over his glasses at the men who had come into the room, and said in his high, nasal tone, 'This court is now in session.'

The sheriff reddened. He considered that Lister Crane had far outlived his usefulness, if—which he doubted—the judge had ever had any usefulness. But he had learned from past experience to treat this old gadfly with respect, and he said now with a show of humility he did not feel, 'This is only a preliminary hearing, Your Honor. I arrested this same man the other night, and you turned him loose on a writ because you said that I

187

had not brought him in for a proper preliminary hearing.'

Lister Crane looked at Belmont with shrewd old eyes, his nutcracker face expressionless, his bluish lips looking tight and uncompromising.

'Don't you know enough not to come in here wearing guns?'

Belmont nodded. 'Your Honor,' there was nothing in his manner to show any feeling, 'I did not mean to insult this court by coming in here armed. Unfortunately, had I not worn my guns, I might not have gotten here.' As he spoke, he reached down and unfastened his gunbelt and, stepping forward, placed it on the corner of Crane's desk.

Crane, of course, knew the full story of what had been happening in the basin. It was impossible not to know, but it was necessary that he consider only evidence which was brought before him in his capacity as judge.

'Well, what are you here for?'

Belmont shrugged and looked at the sheriff. Glass' face had deepened in color. He wished that Ab Sellers were present to tell him what to do. He glanced at the doorway in time to see Helen enter, followed by the mountain girl, but there was no sign of Sellers.

He said, 'This man killed Charles Ronson, known as Bronc Charley.'

'Huh.' Crane studied Belmont as if he were some rare specimen. 'Killed him, huh?

Where's the complaining witness?'

The sheriff's face had a confident expression. 'He isn't here, but I have a statement he signed.' He produced a folded paper. 'Do you want me to read it?'

The judge snorted. 'Still able to read myself.' He extended a thin hand, took the paper and peered at it. 'Shot him, huh? Okay, young fellow, what you got to say about this?'

Belmont described the fight in a low voice.

'Got any witnesses?'

Belmont nodded to the boy who had been standing quietly at his side. The judge grunted. 'Kind of young, ain't he?'

The sheriff stirred himself. He said in an angry, protesting tone, 'Naturally you know this boy will back up anything that Belmont says. His father was a stage-robber, and he himself knows where that stolen gold is hidden. Surely you can't take his word against that of a respectable business man?'

The judge peered at him, and the sheriff reddened. He wished again that Ab Sellers were here to tell him what to do.

Crane looked at Davey. 'All right. You tell it, son.'

Davey told him. His voice was low and bitter. He told it all from the time of his father's hanging and his mother's death by the Apaches, told of Belmont's help and how Belmont had arrived when Bronc Charley and Honest John were trying to make him tell where the gold was hidden.

Belmont glanced around as he listened, and was surprised to find that the courtroom behind him had filled up. He had not been conscious of people's arrival, he had been so intent on the judge.

He heard Crane say finally, 'Too bad you haven't got another witness. I kind of believe you, Dave, but I'll have to bind Belmont over for the grand jury.'

'But there is another witness.' The boy's voice cracked a little with excitement. 'Her.' He was pointing at Mary Lu. 'She was hiding in the timber. She saw it all.'

The judge turned to look at the girl. So did the sheriff. So, for that matter, did everyone in the crowded room. Mary Lu Walker was the center of attention, but for all the outward sign she gave she might have been standing alone before the judge.

She told her story in a quiet voice. She told it steadily, and a man less fair-minded than the judge would have been forced to believe her. When she had finished, there was a moment of deep silence in the courtroom. Then someone at the rear started to applaud and the whole room seemed to take it up.

The judge's face went beet-red. He seized his gavel and beat with it upon the desk until the applause died, then he said in a dangerous tone, 'If there is any more disturbance I'll have the courtroom cleared.'

He glared out over the heads of those who stood before him, and afterward he said to Belmont in a milder tone, 'Having these witnesses, I wonder that you did not ride into Stanton and tell your story.'

Belmont met his eyes levelly. 'I'm a stranger,' he said, 'and these two,' he indicated the boy and girl, 'had very little to reassure them of Stanton justice. I'd been arrested once, and thought that I would probably be arrested again, and unfortunate accidents happen to prisoners in the Stanton jail.'

The judge's expression did not change. Belmont did not know how he would accept the words. He stared for another long instant at Belmont, then turned his attention to the sheriff.

'I find no evidence here sufficient to hold this man for trial.' He said this calmly, distinctly. 'If you still feel that there is evidence enough, you can sign the arrest warrant and take him before a grand jury, but I warn you that you will not get a true bill.'

Barney Glass looked a little helplessly at the man behind the desk. Without Ab Sellers to guide him he was at sea.

The judge gave him a moment longer, then looked at Davey Berry. 'This boy is, I understand, an orphan?'

Belmont roused himself. 'If it please, Your Honor, I will gladly take the boy with me.'

191

Crane's eyes seemed to narrow. 'It doesn't please us,' he said. 'The boy by rights is a ward of the court, and as such this court does not feel that his best interests will be served by accompanying a drifter down the trail. Do you have a home, a place to take him?'

Slowly Belmont shook his head, but his mouth was set in a stubborn line. 'I don't, but if he stays here what has he got to look forward to? Who will take care of him? Ever since they hung his father, everyone here and everyone in Toprock has watched him with only one thought in mind—that he might lead them to the hiding place of the gold stolen from that stage.' He paused to throw a glance at the angry sheriff.

'Do you expect Glass to look after the boy? I ask you, has he made any effort to locate the men who lynched the boy's father?'

Glass seemed to swell with gathering anger. He said contemptuously, 'Dave Berry was a thief, a rustler and a no-good bum.'

The boy twisted, his thin face looking very dangerous, but Belmont grasped one shoulder, steadying him.

The judge was frowning at the sheriff. He said clearly, 'I don't believe that Dave Berry stood trial?'

Glass glared back a little uncertainly. 'Everyone knew he was guilty. Why, he didn't deny it. It was common talk and . . .'

The judge's voice was like the crack of a

whip. 'Our law,' he said, and he seemed to grow inches while he was speaking, 'assumes that every man is innocent until he has been found guilty. Therefore, at the time of his death Dave Berry was innocent in the eyes of the law and entitled to the protection which our law provides. You should have provided that protection.'

The sheriff shifted his big bulk first to one foot, and then to the other. He tried to look the judge in the eye, but wound up staring at the floor between his booted feet. 'I had nothing to do with it.' The words were muttered in so low a tone that those at the back of the courtroom could not hear.

But the judge heard and he bristled, his voice nearly submerged by his gathering anger. 'I know the story of Berry's death. It's been told on every street corner and in every saloon in town. I know that you weren't at the jail when it happened, that six men broke in and took the prisoner out and hung him. I also know that it's been whispered about town that they actually did not mean him to die, that they hoped to scare him into talking. But he did die. It was murder, and I call upon you as the law enforcement officer of this county to tell this court exactly what steps you have taken to apprehend those men.'

There was dead silence in the courtroom. You could have heard a fly land upon the judge's bench. There was no one in the room, the sheriff included, who did not know that the raid on the jail had been made by six Box S riders under the command of Joe Moss. There was also no one in the room, with the exception of Belmont, the boy and Mary Lu, who was not certain that the raid had been carried out on the express orders of Ab Sellers.

The fact that Sellers had taken no direct part in the hanging made little difference. He had sat in his hotel room, probably watching from the window as they took the hapless Berry down to the bridge on which the railroad spanned the Black River, and there, on the sandy bank beside the smoothly running stream, had thrown the rope over the stringer and hoisted Berry until only his toes touched.

'Answer me.' It was the judge. Everyone in the courthouse had forgotten that he was a small man. He completely dominated the scene.

The sheriff was like a wounded bear, shifting first this way and then that, looking for an avenue of escape and finding none. 'Lemme alone.' The words broke out of him. He was feeling hugely put upon. He had only done what almost every citizen of Stanton would have done in his place. He had taken orders from Ab Sellers.

Judge Crane pretended to be surprised. He could be vastly sarcastic when he chose, and

194

he chose now. He said with raised eyebrows, 'Surely our sheriff who is brave enough to chase a fifteen-year-old boy isn't afraid to go after half a dozen lynchers?'

Barney Glass had very little defense against a man like Crane. He was slow-witted, a plodder, honest enough according to his own lights, and he was feeling very much aggrieved.

'I ain't afraid of no one.' He said this loudly, glaring around as if daring someone in the room behind him to dispute it. 'But I ain't going to make a fool of myself either. If you want those men brought in, supposing you go out and bring them in yourself, Judge.'

Crane looked at him with unblinking eyes. 'Sheriff,' he said, 'it looks to me as if you are refusing to do your duty. You don't leave me any choice but to wire the territorial governor and ask for your removal.'

Barney Glass was not afraid of anything he thought Crane could do. He had abiding faith in Ab Sellers' power. He felt that as long as he had Ab Sellers at his back he could face down Crane, yes, and the governor as well.

'You go to the devil,' he said and, turning, started to push his way out through the crowd.

'Wait a minute.' Crane's voice had lost none of its whip-like qualities. 'You probably don't know enough about the law to realize that my hands are not completely tied. There are certain things I can do if the local officers refuse to cooperate. This is, for your information, a federal court and, since this is a territory rather than a state, a number of things come under my jurisdiction which would not be true if it were a state. Also, this court rates a marshal and as many deputies as I think are necessary. I've never before been faced with a situation which I thought the local law officers could not handle, but I am now. I give you one more chance to produce those lynchers—otherwise I'll appoint a marshal to do the job for you.'

Barney Glass swung back. His eyes were hot and intolerant. 'You old fool!' he said. 'There isn't a man in the whole of Stanton who would wear your badge, or who would live two hours after he pinned it on.' He glared at the judge for a moment, then turned his back and stomped out of the courtroom.

Crane watched him go, waiting until the door had slammed behind his retreating back, then he said, 'Unfortunately, there is some truth in what our noble sheriff says. We are, it seems, very near the edge of civilization. There are, I believe, five under-strength companies of cavalry in the whole territory, and these are much too busy chasing Indians to be at all concerned with civilian matters.'

He paused, his eyes going out across the courtroom as if considering possibilities. 'Are there any volunteers?'

No one stirred, not even a foot moved. It

was as if the spectators hoped to pass unnoticed, and wanted to do nothing which would call attention to their presence.

Belmont had listened, a hint of humor quirking the corners of his mouth, listened in detachment. The judge calling his name brought him back to the present with a start.

'Belmont.'

'Sir?' The form of address was instinctive. He had been highly impressed by this small fiery man behind the desk.

'You'll do.'

For an instant he did not realize what Crane meant. Then he shook his head in quick protest. 'No, not me. I'm a stranger here. This is not my business.'

'It is your business. It is every man's business who believes in law and order.'

The thought brought an added quirk to Belmont's mouth. Never in his life had he considered that he stood for law and order. He had not been an outlaw, not in the sense that he had robbed and killed for profit, but he had always had the cowboy's feeling that a law officer was a kind of natural enemy put there to stop him in his search for pleasure.

He said slowly, trying to make his point clear, 'I'm a stranger in this country, and if you appoint me you may do more harm than good. People don't like strangers coming in sporting badges and telling them what to do. You don't seem to have many friends here,

197

Judge, and if you were to appoint me you'd have fewer.'

'Are you afraid?'

Belmont considered this. Only a fool had never been afraid. There were situations which would bring a natural terror to any ordinary man.

He said, 'Probably, but that isn't the reason I'm refusing. I just figure that if I took on this chore I'd do more harm than I would good.'

The judge seemed to recognize defeat, but he did not give up. He said slowly, 'I was interested in the story the boy told, how you came to his aid, how you refused to ride away and leave him to face the basin alone. I'm not a fool. I think I can see what was in your mind. You didn't stay because you liked him, but because you figured that he deserved a chance and that he wasn't getting it.

'All right. I'm offering you a chance. There is a point in every man's life when he has a choice, and if he fails to make the right one he regrets it for the rest of his days. I know. I had a choice like that to make once. Take up your guns and bring in these men, then if you want to ride on, ride, and the boy can go with you.'

He stopped, and the gathering noise in the courtroom died, and Belmont stood, his big body hunched a little, his head bent. He turned slightly and saw Davey Berry staring up at him, and saw the hunger in the boy's eyes, and thought—if I ride away now he'll think

I'm no good, and anything he's learned will be lost.

Slowly, as if his hand moved without orders from his brain, he reached out to lift the worn gunbelt from the desk. Behind him he heard a sharp-drawn breath, and then a swell of excited murmuring.

He fastened the belt around his thin hips. He lifted his head and looked squarely at the judge. 'I'm not much at figuring things out,' he said, 'but I'll do the best I can.' He turned then and found Davey at his side, the young face eager.

'I'll help you.'

Belmont looked at him for a long moment. 'Davey,' he said, 'the first thing a kid has to learn is to take orders. I can't have you underfoot in this. You stay with the judge while it's going on. If you don't, I wash my hands of the whole business. I'll ride out.'

He read disappointment and rebellion in the boy's eyes. His own were cold, a little bleak-looking. He said tersely, 'That's the way it is.'

The crowd was moving out of the courtroom, pushing in their rising hurry to tell their fellows what had happened. He came face to face with Helen Sellers and stopped. They stood thus for one long moment looking at each other, and he said finally, 'You don't approve?'

She answered in a low voice, steadily, 'I

199

don't know. I don't disapprove. I'd have been disappointed had you done anything else. But I can't forget it was my father who ordered the hanging.'

19.

Helen Sellers came out of the courtroom with Mary Lu at her side. She was curiously shaken, and so intent on her own thoughts that she hardly noticed the excited comment of the crowd as they thronged around her.

She moved down the sidewalk to the hotel and climbed the steps without noticing Claude Wolfson, who stood watching her from the far end of the porch.

'Helen.'

She stopped at the sound of his voice, hesitated, and then would have moved on.

'I want to talk to you.' He did not come forward. He just stood there, watching her.

She was undecided, then, recognizing that this was a necessity which could not be avoided, she turned to the girl at her side, saying in a tone too low to reach Wolfson, 'Wait for me inside, honey.'

Mary Lu looked at her doubtfully, then turned into the lobby of the hotel.

Helen Sellers turned and came along the porch between the split-backed rockers. She said in an even tone, 'We'd better sit down and talk quietly unless you want to attract the attention of the whole street.'

He smiled, his even teeth making a white line in the darkness of his suntanned face, and the magnetism of his personality which had attracted her in the first place was very strong. She was conscious of it, and she knew suddenly what had not dawned upon her before—that it was something Wolfson could turn on or off at will, according to his purpose.

It brought a further disillusionment which shocked her, and she thought—what if Belmont had not come? What if none of this trouble had developed? What if I had married Claude without learning the shallowness of his appeal?

She shuddered, drawing a long measured breath at the closeness of her escape. 'You wanted to talk to me?' Her voice was not quite steady, and Wolfson mistook the cause.

He himself was discovering that this girl held more appeal for him than he had realized. He had always considered her first as the heir to Ab Sellers' ranches, but now he knew that he wanted her for herself, for her attractiveness, for her effect upon him, and the knowledge only increased his bitterness.

He said evenly, 'I hope you realize how your actions of the last two days will be looked on by the basin.'

She stared at him, startled. 'Looked on by

the basin?'

He said tensely, 'I'm not meaning to criticize, and I realize that you were trying to be humane in helping the boy and Belmont, but I'll have to ask that you be a little more careful after we are married.'

She said slowly, distinctly, 'We aren't going to be married, Claude.'

Her words, half expected, still came with jarring force. He controlled himself with an effort and, reaching across, took her arm, his fingers biting through the fabric of her sleeve.

'Listen to me. We are going to be married.'

'Let go.' She had not moved, but her eyes had some of the quality of command he had seen in her father's.

'But . . .'

'Let me go.'

Slowly he withdrew his hand. She rose then, standing above him, saying in a low voice, 'I made a mistake, Claude. I'm not blaming you. I don't blame others for my mistakes. I know now that I didn't love you, that I was coming to you merely as a gesture to defy my father.'

'The drifter?' He rose now and some of his hard-held anger broke through. 'You'll never marry him—that I promise you.'

She said, 'It isn't Belmont. It's me, and you. You aren't the person I thought you were, Claude—the one I imagined you were. But tell me one thing. Why did you send your men to trap Belmont and the boy? What was it you wanted? The gold?'

He opened his mouth to protest, to say that he had not sent them, that it had been Doane's idea, but she did not wait. She had turned and was moving quickly along the length of the dusty porch. A moment later she vanished through the door to the lobby.

He stood for minutes staring down the street. A knot of men had gathered before the saloon, and he saw the tall figure of the new marshal standing there talking to them. He turned then and followed the girl into the lobby.

By the time he arrived the place was empty. There was no one in sight. He climbed the stairs. He did not head for his own room, or for that of the girl. Instead, he went back along the hall to the big square room at the rear which Sellers always occupied. He knocked.

There was a moment's silence and then the rancher's voice. 'Come in.'

Wolfson pushed open the door. Sellers was at a kind of desk he had fashioned for himself out of the washstand. Wolfson stopped, and for a long moment these two men who had never been friends measured each other. Then Wolfson moved forward, closing the door quietly behind him.

'It's time,' he said, 'that we had a talk.'

Sellers did not answer. He continued to watch Wolfson.

203

'You know what happened at the courthouse?'

The movement of Sellers' head was so slight that it could hardly be called a nod.

'Belmont is now a federal marshal. Belmont has orders to bring in the men who hung Dave Berry.'

The old man said, 'He'll never make it.'

'You're a fool,' Wolfson told him, and watched the red of anger come up under the tan of Sellers' face. 'This town hates you. There's hardly a person in it who won't cheer to see you locked up. The only reason they haven't moved against you is that they are afraid. But Belmont isn't afraid, and your crew is strung out from hell to breakfast. It will be tomorrow or the next day before you could call them all in.'

He saw by Sellers' eyes that the man agreed.

'So I'm here to offer you a deal. I'll take care of friend Belmont. I've already sent for my men. But I want to be paid for doing it.'

'How paid?' Sellers had drawn a small cigar from his shirt pocket and was staring at it thoughtfully.

'You're old,' said Wolfson. 'And you have no son. I want a partnership. I want to throw our ranches together. Between us we can control the whole basin.'

'And my daughter?' The older man's eyes were shrewd.

204

'That will come.' Wolfson spoke with more confidence than he felt. 'Leave that part to me.'

Sellers rose slowly, and suddenly Wolfson knew how tired the rancher was and how the pressures of the last few days had borne in on him, and he knew that Sellers would agree, that Sellers would agree to almost anything.

'Get rid of Belmont,' he said. 'Get control of the town, and then we'll talk.'

Wolfson was not quite satisfied, but he knew Sellers well enough to know that you could not push the old man too far too fast.

'I'll do it,' he said. 'Belmont won't be around to see tomorrow's sun come up.'

20.

Wearing the marshal's badge, Ross Belmont came out of the courthouse and moved slowly down the street. He had a sensation of being alone, which seemed strange, since the greater portion of his life had been spent without companionship of any kind.

But always before he had been one of the nameless crowd. Now he realized that he was a man apart, and that everyone on the street watched his progress with veiled but active interest. He came abreast of the saloon and saw the men who were grouped around its

205

door, and crossed the street's thick cushion of dust to step up onto the walk and face them.

He heard their conversation die and studied their unresponsive faces. It was not hostility they felt, but an uncertain reserve. He was a stranger to them, and as such someone who could not be trusted too far.

He said quietly, 'You all know who I am and why I'm here and why Judge Crane saw fit to pin this badge upon my shirt. It's a job I did not want, and one which came to me by default. This is your town, not mine, and it is important to all of you who live here to help make the law work.'

He tried to read acceptance in their faces and found none.

'A man was hung,' he said, 'a man who had no friends. But that man might well be any of you, and if nothing is done about his hanging, the act of violence might well be repeated.'

Tom Flynn owned the harness shop. Tom Flynn was big and slow-thinking and cautious, but he was not afraid. He said in his heavy voice, 'What is it you want from us?'

'The names of the men who hung Dave Berry.'

Flynn turned this over in his mind. He knew who the men in the party had been. He knew they were Sellers' riders, led by Joe Moss. He knew this as nearly everyone in Stanton knew it. But he had himself to think of, and his family, and he knew that no business could

206

exist for long in the basin if the owner drew the displeasure of Ab Sellers.

He said slowly, 'Anyone in town can tell you who they were, but I doubt that anyone will— not openly. And if you do find out you'll never take them.'

'I'll take them,' Ross Belmont said. He said it simply, quietly, and it was his quiet confidence which impressed Tom Flynn.

Flynn glanced at the men around him, knowing that they were not friends of Sellers, yet not trusting them, then he moved his big shoulders in a shrug of resignation.

'A man needs to live with himself.' He was talking to no one in particular, justifying his action only to himself. 'It was Ab Sellers' men,' he said, and felt the group stir around him. 'Sellers ordered it. You can bet on that. But Sellers himself was not with the party. Joe Moss led them.'

Several men released their breaths, as if they had been holding them too long, and there was a sudden air of expectancy within the group which had not been there a moment before. And then behind them came the hard drum of hoofs upon the road from the west, and half a dozen of Wolfson's men pounded down the street to pull up before the livery stable.

Ross Belmont saw them come, recognizing Ben August, although he did not know his name, and turned to glance up and down the sidewalk for a sight of Wolfson and failed to see him.

He was at once alert. Some of these men had helped attack him on the canyon rim, and he did not believe that their arrival here in town was accidental.

But they made no move toward him. They rode to the livery, dismounting and unsaddling their horses to turn them into the corral. This in itself should have warned him, for it was apparent that they meant to stay in town some while. He waited until they came from the livery and passed on the far side of the street, moving up toward the hotel. Then with a muttered word of thanks to Flynn he retraced his steps and re-entered the courthouse.

It was growing late, and the room in which the judge sat with the boy was deep in shadow, although outside the building the light still held.

Dave jumped up as Belmont came in, but Ross ignored him, walking down until only the desk separated him from the judge.

He said in his quiet voice, 'Too many people around when you pinned this on me,' he indicated the badge with a small flick of his finger, 'for us to talk much.'

The judge did not answer.

'Seems everyone in town but me knows exactly who is guilty. The sheriff just rode out as I left here, going somewhere in a hurry.'

'To see Sellers,' the judge suggested.

208

'Sellers is in town at the hotel. That's what I came back about. It seems he ordered the hanging, but he wasn't there in person. The men who slung the rope are out in the hills somewhere hunting me.' His mouth quirked a little. 'Point is, do I bring Sellers in? I don't know much about the law, but if he ordered the hanging I'd think he was responsible.'

'That will have to be proved.'

'Proving isn't my part,' Belmont told him gently. 'Should be a lawyer to do that. But if Sellers is locked up, maybe the other boys will come in more easy, or else clear out of the country.'

'Bring him in.'

'That's what I wanted to know.' He glanced at the boy for a long moment of silence, then turned on his heel and went out of the room.

His progress up the street in the gathering dusk was marked by a hundred eyes, but no one watched him with more intentness than Claude Wolfson, who stood just inside the hotel lobby watching through the window.

His men were behind him and he turned, saying in a tight, sharp voice, 'He's coming here. He must be coming after Sellers.'

Ben August grinned, showing his broken teeth. 'He'll get a hotter reception than he expects.'

'Not too fast.' Wolfson was thinking. 'Ben, you and I will slip upstairs and into my room. It's at the front end of the hall. Sellers' is at the rear. We'll wait until the marshal knocks on Sellers' door, until Sellers answers, then we'll get him.'

August showed his dislike of the idea. 'Why not take him down here? We're seven-to-one.'

Wolfson's voice was suddenly whip-like. 'Don't any of you ever use your heads? The man may be a saddle tramp, but he's wearing a U. S. marshal's badge. We down him, and Sellers claims he knew nothing of it and turns against us, and what happens? That crackpot judge will bring in all the law the government can dig up. No, we wait until Sellers is facing him and then we yell, and when he swings around we get him from in front. Then we both swear that it was Ab Sellers who did the shooting, resisting arrest.'

August grinned his understanding.

'The rest of you get into the dining room and close the door. When you hear the shot, come busting up the stairs.'

They nodded and turned toward the side room. Wolfson led August up the stairs and along the hall. They had barely reached his room when Belmont thrust open the lobby door and came in.

He paused for a moment as he saw that the room was empty, then moved its length to punch the hand-bell on the high desk. The clerk appeared almost at once from the small office in the rear, and stared with deepening curiosity at this stranger wearing the badge.

'Which is Ab Sellers' room?'

'Well, he . . .'

'Which is it?' The cool eyes seemed to bore through the clerk.

He gulped once, then said in a weak voice, 'It's the door at the back end of the upper hall. You can't miss it.'

Belmont offered no thanks. He went up the stairs easily, softly, despite the aching tiredness in his long muscles. He stopped at the head of the steps, looking one way and then the other along the hall. All the doors were closed and no sound reached his ears.

He moved forward then to stop and knock on Sellers' door, and waited as steps came toward him across the room and the door was pulled inward, exposing the rancher.

'Oh, it's you.'

Belmont said, 'You know why I'm here, Mr. Sellers. Get your hat. We're going down to the jail . . .'

He never got an answer, for behind him from the front of the hall he heard Wolfson's voice.

'Belmont. Wait a minute.'

Wolfson expected him to turn. Wolfson's gun was up and ready, but Wolfson counted without one thing. Belmont had seen the Wolfson crew ride in and make for the hotel, and he had been wondering where they were ever since he stepped into the building.

He reached out, caught the edge of the

doorjamb and with a single motion pulled himself around it, squeezing into the room between Sellers' thin body and the door. He was almost out of sight before Wolfson realized what had happened, and then Wolfson's reflexes took over and he squeezed the trigger of the heavy gun in his hand. The slug which had been meant for Belmont struck Ab Sellers directly in the chest. The shocking force of the 255-grain bullet carried the small rancher back almost to the center of the room before he fell.

Belmont had made a complete turn and his gun was in his hand. He leaned around the edge of the door and fired at Wolfson and missed, the bullet passing Wolfson's side to smash full into the stomach of Ben August.

He fired again, and then the pound of feet coming up the stairs warned him that the rest of Wolfson's crew were taking a hand, and he slammed the door, shoving the light bolt into place. Outside the door there was turmoil. He heard Wolfson's high shout.

'He shot Ab! He killed Sellers!' and his mouth settled into a tight, grim line. They were muttering out there in the hall, hesitating to attack the door, since he could easily shoot them through the light panels. He wasted no time.

There was a window at the rear of the room, already open, the stained curtains blowing a little with the evening breeze. He crossed the room on silent feet and had one leg over the sill when the shot came, the bullet tearing its way through the flimsy door.

He fired in return, twice, merely to hold them for a moment, then slipped the other leg out and lowered himself until he hung from the window ledge by his fingertips. Then he dropped, landing unshaken in the dust coat of the alley. There was an old barn across the alley and he made around it, pausing as he gained its shelter to breathe deeply.

He did not linger. It was still not entirely dark, and he knew that any movement he made would be witnessed from the windows of the hotel, but he had to take the chance, sprinting across an open place to a row of cabins which straggled along the edge of a side street.

He had almost reached them when a gun cracked from the window he had just left, and a bullet buried itself in the thick logs. Then he was around the corner of the cabin and, for the moment, safe.

21.

Darkness deepened like a protective blanket, a darkness which Belmont welcomed as a rescuing friend. He had crossed the side street and found shelter in a small shed which was

213

open at both ends. He would not trust himself in a building which did not offer a quick exit, and he wanted a place to remain out of sight for the long minutes until the night was thick enough to cover his movements.

He was not too worried for the immediate future. Wolfson's men would be cautious in their search, knowing that he was armed, and unless some chance citizen had seen him reach the shed and relayed the information they did not know where he was.

But the odds were great. Six men had ridden in, and he had hit Ben August. This meant that with Wolfson there would still be six to hunt him down. And he expected no help from the townsmen. Their attitude before the saloon had told plainer than any words that they were not about to take an active hand in this battle. The harness maker, perhaps, but no one else.

Outside it was now full dark. Only the sky toward the west still carried its suggestion of light, as the afterglow of the setting sun showed in reflection above the high mountain peaks.

He shifted a little, wondering what he should do. The obvious thing was to get a horse and ride out. The odds were great, and Ab Sellers was dead. The thought made him remember the girl.

She had gone out of her way to help him twice, and, although she had had differences with her father, he still remembered how she had looked in the courtroom when she told him that her father was responsible for the hanging. It was almost as if the heart were being torn out of her, and he knew a sudden gladness that it had been Wolfson's bullet, not his, which had killed the rancher.

The thought of Wolfson tightened his mouth. If his fight was with anyone it was with Wolfson, and the fact that he could not quite understand the man's actions only served to heighten his anger.

No, he would not run. He'd stay until the job was finished. He had run enough. He rose from the bench on which he had been resting and peered out at the pattern of the town. There were no lights on the streets, the only illumination coming from the lamps which showed through the windows of the stores and houses.

Cautiously, he left the shed and eased down the side street toward the main thoroughfare. He reached the corner where the Sellers bank stood, and had a moment to wonder who would run it now that the old man was dead. He peered around it and was surprised to see no activity on the sidewalk.

And then he realized that he was the reason for its being deserted—he and Wolfson. The people of Stanton were trying to stay neutral in this fight, and he could expect no help from them.

He stood, trying to picture what Wolfson would do, how he would set up his crew, and decided that they would be ranged along Main Street, watching for him to try and cross.

That's what he would have done if he had been in Wolfson's shoes. Wolfson would assume that Belmont, being alone, would try to escape from town. In order to escape he would need a horse, and all the horses were at the livery on the far side of Main Street.

If he needed something to confirm his theory, the absence of horses along the racks should have told him that he was right, for there was not a single pony in sight. Apparently, Wolfson's men had led them to the barn out of harm's way.

His mouth set. Not that for a second he had really considered leaving, but because this showed the care they were going to to hunt him down. If he only knew where Wolfson was. Would the man wait at the livery, expecting him to make a try for a horse?

And then he saw a man shift along the shadows under the wooden awning to his right. He gripped his gun, creeping carefully forward. If he could get close eriough to ram his gun against the man's back, to make him talk, to find out where Wolfson was.

But he never got close enough. He was still a hundred feet away when a second figure came out of a dark doorway to say in a low voice, 'Any sign of him?'

216

'None. He hasn't tried to reach a horse yet, but he will. He'll have to get out of town before daylight.'

'Wolfson still at the saloon? I could use a drink myself.'

'You'll get one when this is over, not before.' He moved on, but Belmont no longer followed. Instead, he faded back into the shadows, rounding the corner thankfully, and edged back along the side street, watchful. Not all Wolfson's men might be on Main Street.

But he came without challenge to the bisecting alley and turned into it, moving along its length with purpose until he reached the rear door which gave on the saloon.

Here he paused, debating. The door was paneled, with no glass opening, and the windows in the wall were set so high that it was impossible for him to see into the room beyond.

He hated to enter the saloon blind. It was like walking into a trap, but he had no choice. Certainly, he could not hope to go in through the Main Street door.

He reached out with his left hand and gently turned the knob, more than expecting to find that the door was locked. It wasn't, but the door stuck a little. He put steady pressure on it, praying that any noise he made would not be noticed by those within. The door gave, and he pushed it open

217

gingerly, peering into the room beyond.

Wolfson and two of his men stood at the front end of the bar, turned sidewise so that their backs were toward Belmont as they watched the street beyond the dirty windows with concentrated attention.

Belmont was in the room before they heard him. The only other occupant of the place, the bartender, saw him first. His eyes went wide with startled fright, and without a sound he ducked down behind the heavy counter.

Wolfson turned, his men coming about with him, and the three of them stood thus, staring for an instant at Belmont as if he had been a man from another planet.

Belmont's gun was in his holster. He had had it in his hand when he came through the door, but as soon as he realized that they weren't facing him and that their guns were in their belts, he dropped his gun back into the leather.

He knew enough about Wolfson to judge that the man would not attempt to draw if Belmont already held his gun in his hand. Wolfson would dissemble, putting off the showdown until the cards were more in his favor. And Belmont did not want it put off. He realized that there could be no ending to this as long as they both lived. But even so, he gave Wolfson a small chance to back out.

'You're under arrest,' he said quietly.

This, Wolfson had not expected. The shock

of seeing Belmont behind him, when he had been certain in his own mind that somewhere the man was trying to cross the dark street, was almost physical. It held him paralyzed for the barest instant, then he recovered, conscious that the men on each side of him had shifted slightly so that a little space was between them, so that they all had a certain freedom of action.

'For what?' The words were squeezed out of Wolfson by his surprise.

'For interfering with an officer who was trying to make an arrest—for shooting at me—for killing Sellers.'

Wolfson grinned suddenly, cat-like. 'Killing Sellers?' He managed to sound surprised. 'Why, the whole town knows you went up to his hotel room and shot him.'

The words struck Belmont with complete surprise. It had not entered his head that he, rather than Wolfson, would be blamed for Sellers' death, and then he realized that there had been no other witnesses to the shooting except Wolfson and August, and August was dead.

He knew a temptation to glance at the bartender. He guessed that Wolfson had spoken now for the man's benefit, but he had to keep watching Wolfson, and then thought of Helen Sellers and his mouth tightened. Probably she too believed that he had killed her father.

219

Wolfson saw Belmont's surprise and chose the moment to draw, his hand sweeping down in a smooth practiced motion, his curved fingers lifting the gun from its holster. But it was his own men rather than Belmont whom he caught off guard, for Belmont had been watching Wolfson's eyes, and he saw them crystallize with purpose.

Even so, Wolfson's gun was free of the leather first, the heavy barrel tipping upward by the time Belmont drew. But Wolfson shot too fast. Nearly fifteen feet separated them, and the short-barreled gun had been made for closer work. The slug struck the top of the bar on Belmont's left, plowing a groove along the marred surface and going out through the room's rear wall.

Belmont took his time. He brought his gun up slowly and fired just as Wolfson squeezed off his second shot. This time Wolfson did not miss. His bullet struck Belmont in the upper left leg, tearing through the fleshy tissue without touching the bone.

But Belmont had not missed either. His single shot had caught Wolfson directly in the chest, sending him backward against one of his men who, in the act of drawing, was knocked off balance.

Belmont went down just as the second Wolfson crewman got his gun free. He fired, too high, the bullet cutting the air above Belmont.

Belmont shot him through the head, and he fell. The other rider had had enough. He threw a shot at Ross and then turned and ran through the door; sending the batwings flapping by his passage.

For a moment, the saloon was blanketed in heavy silence, then the bartender stuck his head up above the counter cautiously. His eyes met Belmont's as Ross, putting one hand on the bar, managed to drag himself upward to his feet. He stood on his good leg, balancing for a moment, then his eyes fell on the shotgun against the backbar.

'Hand me that.'

The bartender gave it to him silently.

'Now, blow out the lights.'

The man hesitated, as if not wishing to leave the shelter of the bar. Slowly he came around, lowering the big center lamp, and blew it out. Then, in the resulting darkness, he scuttled for the back door like a hurrying crab, letting the door bang behind him as he disappeared into the blackness of the alley.

Belmont was motionless, his eyes adjusting to the gloom, his every sense alert, the double-barreled gun held firmly in his hand. He heard voices on the street and then the sound of hurrying feet, and afterward the rush of horses, and he guessed rather than knew that the fleeing puncher had carried the word to his companions that Wolfson was dead. They were pulling out. The fight was over.

It was only a few minutes, but it seemed like an hour before the townsmen came edging in, uncertain, to see what had happened. He stood in the center of the group, with the judge before him, and listened to the judge congratulate him. And then above their heads he saw Helen Sellers come in through the door, followed by Mary Lu and Davey.

The crowd parted as if by instinct and let the girl come through, and she stood for a long moment facing him before she came forward to stand silently, looking at him as if to assure herself that he was all right.

He searched her face, not knowing what to say. He was nervous, much more nervous than he had ever been in his life. 'I'm sorry about your father.' He said it in a low voice. 'I . . . he . . . Wolfson told the town that I shot him, but I didn't. It was a kind of accident. Wolfson shot at me and hit him.'

He was watching her face, fearing the disbelief that might be mirrored there, but she surprised him by saying, 'I know. Mary Lu and I were in my room. We heard you come down the hall and I opened the door a crack to see. I . . . I saw what happened.'

He was staring at her, knowing a relief which he could not express. It was so great that he even forgot the ache in his wounded leg. He heard Helen say, 'It's all over. I'll get rid of the full crew, even the ones who had nothing to do with Dave Berry's death. We'll take Davey and Mary Lu out to the ranch. We'll give them a chance, the chance they never had.'

He knew in a dazed way that her 'we' included him, and knew suddenly that the words he had been trying to find need never be spoken, that the understanding between them was more powerful than any words.

He glanced at Mary Lu, and then at the boy. Dave's face was shining. Dave said, 'It's all right, Ross, everything is all right. I told the Judge where the gold is hidden. It's in the livery stable, in the back stall. Pop hid it under the hay bales. I should have told you sooner.'

'It's all right,' said Helen Sellers, and she put one arm about the boy's shoulders and drew him tight. 'We understand, don't we, Ross?'

'Yes,' Ross Belmont agreed. It was all he could say at the moment, with the people crowding around, and yet there was so much that he wanted to tell her, things which he had never said to anyone else.

He winced as the doctor bent down to examine his leg. Well, there would be a lot of time later to talk, a lifetime, but he would have liked the chance to say just three words, I love you. He would have felt a fool, saying them there, before the audience, so he merely smiled, and told her with his eyes.